"I won't pry."

Oh, man... Why did Jack have to be so understanding? He was making it so hard for Ava to just walk away.

"Mama, look!" Missy waved from the top of the platform. Why did they make these playgrounds so high? "I can do it like the big kids."

She leaned out through the gap, and Ava read the intent in her daughter's eyes an instant before she let go and jumped off. "No—Missy!"

The sound of an engine revving reached her just as a dark SUV plowed through the row of bushes, heading straight for them.

Time slowed down. She screamed as she ran for Missy, but there was no way she'd make it.

Jack dove in front of her, grabbing Missy by the arm a split second before she hit the sand. As the truck hit the rock wall she'd been standing on, Jack rolled out of the way with her.

Ava dove to the side to avoid being hit seconds before the truck got caught up in the slide and finally came to a stop.

Deena Alexander grew up in a small town on eastern Long Island where she lived up until a few years ago and then relocated to Clermont, Florida, with her husband, three children, son-in-law and four dogs. Now she enjoys long walks in nature all year long, despite the occasional alligator or snake she sometimes encounters. Her love for writing developed after the birth of her youngest son, who had trouble sleeping through the night.

Books by Deena Alexander

Love Inspired Suspense

Crime Scene Connection
Shielding the Tiny Target

Visit the Author Profile page at LoveInspired.com.

SHIELDING THE TINY TARGET

DEENA ALEXANDER

LOVE INSPIRED SUSPENSE

INSPIRATIONAL ROMANCE

LOVE INSPIRED® SUSPENSE
INSPIRATIONAL ROMANCE

Recycling programs for this product may not exist in your area.

ISBN-13: 978-1-335-58718-3

Shielding the Tiny Target

Love Inspired
22 Adelaide St. West, 41st Floor
Toronto, Ontario M5H 4E3, Canada
www.LoveInspired.com

Printed in U.S.A.

Trust in the Lord with all thine heart;
and lean not unto thine own understanding. In all thy
ways acknowledge him, and he shall direct thy paths.
—*Proverbs* 3:5-6

To Greg, Elaina, Nicholas and Logan—you are my world.

Thank you for always being there for me.

With all my love, forever and always.

ONE

Exhaustion beat at Ava Colburn, and once again her eyes drifted closed.

"Mama." Her three-year-old daughter, Missy, shook her arm. "Play with me."

Ava pulled her reading glasses off and rubbed her eyes. Two hours. She'd spent the last two hours trying to place the flower order for Cara Worthington's sweet sixteen party. "All right, honey. I'm sorry. I just have to finish working, then we'll play something."

"You not working," Missy whined.

Missy's far-too-grown-up pout brought Ava an unexpected smile. She sometimes still couldn't believe how blessed she was. Now if she could just keep her baby safe.

Ava propped the pillows higher against the headboard, slid up farther and shifted the laptop. She inputted her credit card information, then started to read over the order one last time. Finding all of the exotic flowers Cara wanted hadn't been easy. "Of course I'm working, but I'm almost done."

"Then how come your eyes were closed?"

Ava laughed and smoothed the unruly mop of blond

curls. For three, Missy was way too observant. The little girl missed nothing.

Tears shimmered in Missy's bright blue eyes.

With a sigh, Ava closed the computer and set it aside. She'd have to review and submit the order after Missy fell asleep. It was almost ten, and Missy was cranky. She pulled her little girl closer, snuggling under the blanket with her.

Ava loved sharing quiet time with Missy, no matter if it was late at night and Ava hadn't slept well in days. Missy had more energy than she knew what to do with all day long, but nights were different. They could curl up in bed, and Missy would actually stay still long enough to cuddle. With her child's weight against her and the soft scent of baby shampoo enveloping her, Ava closed her eyes.

"Mama." Exasperation filled her child's voice.

Ava's eyes shot open. Missy was not a child you could fall asleep on. "Aww…honey. Why don't we watch a movie?"

Missy shrugged, her lower lip trembling as she tried not to cry. "Princess?"

Ava opened the laptop and pulled it closer, then shuffled through the stack of DVDs on the nightstand.

A soft ding followed by the *you have mail* message made her pause. She dropped a movie into the tray and checked her inbox.

Dear Ms. Colburn,
Due to extenuating circumstances, we've had to cancel Cara's party. I will contact you when or if I wish to reschedule.
Mrs. Worthington

That's it? She scrolled past the signature line. Yup. That was it. No apology, no thank you, no nothing.

"Princess, princess, princess." Missy punctuated each word of the chant with a bounce on the bed.

Nausea threatened. Ava had just wasted all night getting that order together. The first order Marcy, the owner of the flower shop she worked in, had trusted her to do solo. It was supposed to be, Ava knew, her first step toward buying the shop from Marcy, something Marcy was determined to see happen. And, unfortunately, something that could never be, at least not while Ava was living a lie.

She sighed. It could have been worse. At least she hadn't submitted the order. It would have taken the last of the available credit Marcy had allowed her to order all the expensive flowers Cara had insisted on having for her tropical luau. The deposit Mrs. Worthington had left wouldn't have covered even half of them, even if she did keep the money, which she probably wouldn't. It's not like she'd actually ordered the flowers, so all that had been wasted was Ava's time, valuable, but still.

Giving up on getting Ava's attention, Missy stood on the bed and started jumping.

Ava pushed her thoughts aside. She'd call Mrs. Worthington in the morning and make sure she didn't want to reschedule. No sense having to do the order over if she changed her mind…again. And no sense worrying about something she couldn't resolve tonight. Ava hit Play. She massaged her temples, tears tracking down her cheeks. Tears not for the stupid party being canceled, but for the life Missy should have had, the life they'd both been deprived of. Searching for patience, she reached for Missy's hand. "Lay down, baby. Your movie's on."

"Yay. Princess." Missy clapped her hands and bounced up and down then settled against Ava.

Ava's eyelids grew heavy, and she let them close again, only for a moment, as she thought about the past and her husband, Liam. Images of him smiling down at Missy, lifting her in the air for an airplane ride, rocking her in his arms, played through her mind, though none of those things had ever actually happened.

She jerked awake. Something crunched beneath her. What in the world? She rolled over. A rattling noise, just before what felt like shards of glass jabbed into her back. Throwing the covers back, she jumped up. Dozens of little black squares bounced into the space she'd just vacated. She leaned closer, confusion battling the lingering sleepiness. Then her gaze fell on her open laptop. Every key was missing.

Oh, Missy! Apparently, she'd been lost in thoughts of what could have been for more than just a moment. Now she'd spend however long trying to organize the keys and pop them back on, if they'd even stay. She shook out the blanket over the bed as best she could without disturbing Missy, who must have exhausted herself destroying the keyboard and now slept soundly, but she needed something to put the keys in.

With a sigh, and the reluctant acceptance she was doomed to another sleepless night, Ava tiptoed across the room and quietly opened the door. No sense waking Missy when she'd only just—

A noise stopped her in the doorway. She froze, straining to hear past Missy's movie still playing in the background. Something was wrong. The sound of traffic from the nearby highway reached her, not nearly as muffled as it should be if the windows at the back of the house were closed.

Ava backed slowly into the bedroom. How did they find her? She'd been so careful, had eluded them for four years.

Soft footsteps echoed up the stairway. Coming from the kitchen?

She whirled and shut the door quietly. No lock, thanks to Missy locking herself in the room one too many times. Run or call 911? Could she flee out the second story window with Missy before whoever was in the house reached her? She grabbed the phone and dialed. Surely the police in Seaport, New York, would have no way to connect her to a firefighter who was killed in Florida four years ago. If she didn't bring it up, her past should stay buried. Question was, had whoever was in the house made the connection? Or was it just a random break-in? She had to hide Missy.

"Nine-one-one, what is your emergency?"

"Please, I need help," Ava whispered. She started to crawl onto the bed, intent on scooping Missy up. Several laptop keys pierced her hand, and she yanked it back. "Ouch."

The bedroom door creaked open, and she froze. A man's arm came around her neck from behind. He pulled her back against him as he ripped the phone from her hand and disconnected. "Hello, Angelina."

Ava's blood ran cold at the mention of that name, the name she'd left behind four years ago. She braced herself.

"Do not resist me if you want the child to live."

Her gaze fell on Missy still sleeping soundly, and

in that instant, all of the fight drained out of her. She'd never put Missy in danger. And she'd have to stay quiet if she was going to keep her from waking. "Please, can we go into another room? Just leave my daughter sleeping."

Without a word, the man backed toward the doorway, the pressure from his arm threatening to cut off her airway if she didn't move with him. As soon as they reached the hallway, he shoved her to the floor.

Her wrist bent beneath her with a crack. A jolt of pain shot up to her shoulder, robbing her of breath.

"Give me everything you have, and I'll walk away."

She scrambled back a few feet, needing to put some space between them, and beat back the pain. Just because she didn't see a gun, didn't mean he wasn't armed. And he was strong, very strong. Better to just cooperate, bide her time.

If he was demanding what she suspected he was, she didn't have it. And if she did, there was no way he'd let her walk away. "There's a little bit of cash in my purse, but I don't have—"

He grabbed her by the throat and yanked her off the floor. The black ski mask he wore hid all of his features except for his eyes—cold, nearly black eyes that held not an ounce of emotion. "Don't play games with me."

Sirens wailed in the distance.

"I—"

He squeezed tighter, cutting her off, then loosened his grip. "Your husband left something behind when he died. I've already searched his locker at the station, and there's nothing there."

"Please, I don't know what you're talking about." She squeezed her eyes closed and prayed for forgiveness, prayed the last words she uttered wouldn't be a lie. Not that they weren't partially true. When Liam had been killed in the line of duty four years earlier, not from the fire he was fighting but from a gunshot wound he received while fighting the fire, he'd left something behind. At least, she was pretty sure he did based on one of their final conversations, but she didn't know what, and whatever it was, she didn't have it.

"No? Then why did you run? Why have I had to spend the past four years trying to hunt you down?" He jerked her forward, then slammed her head against the wall. "If you had died when we set your house on fire, we could have assumed any evidence died with you, but as it is, well... Not so much."

Spots of light invaded her vision. Only the pain from her wrist dragged her back toward consciousness.

The killer had claimed Liam's life during a fire that wasn't the first in a long series of local arsons in the Florida community where they'd lived. Her husband believed the fires were being deliberately set by a firefighter and covered up. He'd said he had proof, though he didn't say what, but he didn't know who to take it to, who to trust, since he wasn't sure who else was involved.

On the very night Liam had been killed, she'd fled her burning home with a sniper taking shots at her as she ran. "I didn't run. I had to move after my house burned down."

"Yeah, and you just happened to change your name too, right?" The man laughed, but his eyes remained bottomless wells of darkness. "Well, I might have believed that, might even have believed you only fled because I was shooting at you at the time, except that your husband was foolish enough to confide in someone he thought trustworthy on the day he died. I already know he left behind the information—he said so himself, said it was in a safe place with someone he trusted. Since he didn't give it to the police when he contacted them, didn't leave it in his locker, and didn't leave it with his direct supervisor, that leaves you."

Red and blue lights flashed through the front bedroom window and spilled into the hallway.

"Or maybe not. Maybe he left it with a friend, or maybe it did burn to ashes when the house burned down, but the only thing keeping you alive right now is the fact that you probably have what I want, and I need to tie up loose ends so nothing comes out of left field to interfere with our plans. It took four years of searching before the facial recognition program we were using finally paid off when your picture appeared on a blog touting the volunteer work you and that group do at the local hospital."

She should have known better than to try to get involved in the community where she'd settled with Missy, should have known she couldn't give Missy a normal home, a normal life.

"I will not take the chance of losing you again."

A car door slammed.

"Mama?" Missy called from the bedroom. "Mama, I scared. Mama?"

Since Missy tended to have nightmares, she was often scared if she woke alone. Ava prayed Missy would stay where she was and someone would make it in time to save her.

"You have twenty-four hours. If you don't hand over the flash drive, I'll take something precious enough to you to provide sufficient motivation. I'll be watching your every move, and if you try to run or tell the cops what this is about, I'll snatch the child and kill her instead of holding her for ransom."

"Mama? Where are you?" Missy started to cry.

Oh, God, please let her stay put. Please watch over her. Please help us.

Something hard slammed against Ava's head, and she dropped like a stone. An eddy of darkness flooded her peripheral vision. She clung desperately to consciousness.

"To prove I'm serious, and in case the four years since I killed your husband have dulled your memory, I'll leave another firefighter on your doorstep and your conscience as incentive, and remember, it's just as easy to get to someone you love as it is to kill a random stranger who comes to your aid."

No! The wave of black overtook her. Her eyes fluttered closed as she succumbed.

Jack Moretta checked the house number posted on the small ranch's mailbox to be sure it matched that of the woman who'd called nine-one-one, though the gesture was probably unnecessary considering the police cruiser blocking the driveway, then jogged up the walkway and the three steps to the front porch.

Though his living in Seaport was only temporary, at least he could help out while he was there. As a trained firefighter and EMT, volunteering for the local fire and rescue had seemed a logical choice. Plus, he'd be ready to return to his job in New York City when the time came in six months.

A child's screams intruded on his thoughts before

his foot hit the top step. He pounded on the front door, unsure how anyone would hear him over the incessant screaming. "Fire department."

The empty police car sat crookedly in the driveway, its lights still flashing, bathing the quiet block with a blue-and-red strobe effect. Sirens screamed in the distance. Backup wouldn't be far behind, but there was no way he was waiting when dispatch had said the caller was injured and the call had been cut off. Even though police officers had arrived, someone might be in desperate need of medical attention. He hammered his fist against the door. "Fire department."

No answer.

He turned the knob, offering a small prayer of thanks it was unlocked, and pushed the door open, then turned, following the child's screams through the small foyer toward an archway on his right.

"Freeze!" someone said from behind him.

Jack stopped short, put his hands out to the sides and turned to face a police officer who'd come from the other direction and stood on the opposite side of the foyer with his gun trained on Jack. "It's just me, Gabe. I was only a few blocks away at my mom's when the call came in for a woman with a possible injury, and it was quicker to come straight here rather than going to the station first."

"Sorry, Jack, just being careful. We haven't been here long, and we're still searching for the suspect." Gabe holstered his weapon and gestured toward a small living room. "Go ahead in. Ava Colburn and her daughter are on the couch."

As if the screams wouldn't lead him where he needed

to be. He thanked Gabe and poked his head into the living room. "Ava?"

The little girl's screams fell off to soft sobs as she peeked beneath her mother's protective embrace and her gaze fell on him.

A petite woman jumped up from where she'd been sitting on the couch cradling the child. A wild mass of blond curls framed her delicate features, beautiful deep blue eyes narrowed in suspicion. She set the little girl on the couch and stepped in front of her. "Who are you, and what are you doing in my house?"

"Uh…" He'd forgotten this wasn't the city, and the firemen and EMTs here didn't wear uniforms. Instead, volunteers were called in, dropping everything and rushing to the firehouse whenever there was an emergency. Since he'd been home pacing his mother's kitchen, desperate to feel like he was helping her in some way when the call had come in, he ran out without a second thought. At least the call allowed him a distraction from feeling sorry for himself, from questioning God's will.

Well, he might not be able to fix his mother's ailing health, but maybe he could help this woman and her little girl. But in a town this size, where everyone knew everyone else, what must she think of the stranger who'd burst into her living room wearing jeans and a T-shirt? "I'm sorry. I'm new in town."

Her gaze intensified. Blood streamed down the side of her face from a deep cut at her temple and matted in her hair.

Why was he suddenly so tongue-tied? "I mean, I'm with the fire department."

Her stance relaxed, but only a little. She hovered

over the child, who was clearly distressed. "I've never seen you before, and I know most of the firefighters and paramedics in town."

"Like I said, I'm new." He held up his hands in a gesture of surrender. "If you'd like, I can yell for the officer to come in and vouch for me."

A child of about two or three peeked around her mother's side, her big blue eyes red and puffy from crying, her long, thick lashes darkened by tears. The plea in those eyes shot straight to his heart.

Ava eyed him a moment longer, then returned to perch on the edge of the couch cushion. She pulled the little girl back onto her lap. If Jack didn't miss his guess, she was prepared to flee at any moment. With that head injury, he doubted she'd make it far.

He moved toward her slowly, hoping to soothe her, keep her calm, earn her trust. Whatever she'd just been through, he didn't want to make it any worse. "I'm just going to take a look at your head, if that's okay?"

She nodded once but continued to eye him warily, then winced when the little girl shifted. While she hugged the child tightly against her with her right hand, she held her left arm limp against her daughter's back.

"Is your arm hurt too?"

"Who are you?" The little girl, the spitting image of her mother, sniffed and looked up at him.

Oh, man. How could he have forgotten to tell them his name? It could possibly have had something to do with the spunky woman sitting on the couch bleeding, but he pushed that thought away. Definitely not something he needed to think about right now—or ever, if he was smart. "My name's Jack. I'm a fireman."

"Hi." She offered a tentative smile through her tears

and reached a hand up to cradle her mother's cheek. "Mama has a booboo. The bad man did it. He said he's gonna hurt a fireman too. That's what Mama told the policeman. Is the bad man gonna hurt you?"

"The police are here now, baby. He's not going to hurt anyone else." Even as Ava kissed the top of her little girl's head, her eyes darted past him to the closed front door, then skipped to the blind-covered windows.

"But he hurt you," Missy insisted.

Ava pulled the little girl's white-blond curls back from her face and wiped her cheeks. "Shh… Everything will be all right now. Jack will fix me, and everything will be fine. Nobody else is going to get hurt."

The fact that she couldn't keep her gaze still for more than a moment at a time suggested she didn't really believe what she was saying. Was she afraid her attacker would return, or was there something more to her unease? Could the child be right about the intruder threatening to harm a fireman? Was it only a fireman specifically he intended to harm or any rescue worker who came to Ava's aid?

He moved closer and started to examine the wound on Ava's head while he addressed the child. "What's your name?"

Sniff. "Missy."

"It's nice to meet you, Missy." He ran his hands along the sides of Ava's neck. "How old are you?"

"Free an a half." Tears caught and shimmered in her bottom lashes.

"Three and a half, huh?" He smiled, trying to soothe her. "Did the man hurt you too, Missy? Or are you just upset that Mommy's hurt?"

"Umm…" She sucked in a shaky breath. "I scared."

The tears spilled over, and he automatically reached to comfort her, brushing her mother's hand as he did.

Ava pulled her arm away and cradled it against her. "Sorry… I…uh…"

She shook her head. Her knees bounced up and down as if she couldn't sit still. "It's okay."

He finished examining the head wound, which wasn't as bad as he'd originally feared but could definitely use a few stitches. "There's not much I can do until the ambulance gets here with supplies, but I can take a look at your arm. Can you tell me what happened?"

"Someone broke in. He hit me over the head with something and shoved me to the floor." Her uninjured hand shook as she smoothed it over her daughter's hair then tried to shift her aside.

Missy cried and clung to her mother.

He thought of his mother and how upset he'd been when he found out she'd tripped and fallen down the stairs. She hadn't been hurt, but the phone call that followed had brought him out to Seaport, the small town on the south shore of eastern Long Island where he'd grown up, to take care of her until his sister could make more permanent arrangements.

He crouched to meet Missy's stare. "I can't blame you for being upset. Everyone gets upset when someone they love is hurt, but there's nothing to be scared of now, Missy. I'm going to fix your mama all up. And no one's going to hurt you or her as long as I'm here. Okay?"

Missy looked directly into his eyes, almost as if she was searching them for the truth, then nodded and shifted just enough for him to reach her mother's arm.

Ava's wrist had already started to swell, and a nasty bruise had begun to form.

"Can you move it at all?"

She nodded and shifted her hand tentatively back and forth. "I don't think it's broken."

"Still, you should have it looked at and x-rayed when you get to the hospital anyway."

"I'm not going to the hospital." Her gaze darted past him again.

"What? Why not?" He turned and looked over his shoulder, expecting someone to be standing behind him. What was up with her? Was she just jumpy from the intruder? While he couldn't blame her for that, he got the sense there was more than she admitted to her unease, as if she expected something else to happen. "You should really have that head wound checked, at the very least. I'm pretty sure it needs to be stitched."

The little girl had said the intruder intended to harm a fireman. Could that be true, or was she just confused? It seemed like an awfully specific threat. Though he didn't want to ask in front of the child, he couldn't blame her mom for being wary if that was the case. And he certainly intended to be cautious until he could question her further.

She was already shaking her head. "There are bandages in a drawer in the kitchen. I'll just wrap it."

Jack could see the determination in her eyes, and he wasn't about to argue with her. He'd wrap her wrist and bandage her head, then let whoever was on duty take care of coaxing her to go to the hospital. He stood. "At least let me treat you then, so Missy will feel better. Where are the bandages?"

She hesitated a moment, then pointed toward the

archway. "Just go back through there to the kitchen, and open the middle drawer on the center island."

He started toward the foyer.

The front door opened, and one of his fellow fire-fighters stuck his head in and called out, "Hey, Ava, it's Big Earl."

"Big Earl?" Missy yelled.

Big Earl Jensen stepped across the threshold, his customary grin firmly in place, though there was no mistaking the worry in his eyes.

A red dot of light played against the wall, then landed on Big Earl's head.

Missy's warning about a firefighter being hurt played in Jack's head even as he dove toward Earl. "Get down!"

"Huh?" Big Earl started to turn to look over his shoulder.

Jack plowed into him, taking him down and tumbling both of them out the doorway and onto the porch.

A bullet hit the doorjamb where Earl's head had been, splintering the wood.

With one hand on Earl's shoulder to hold him down, Jack scrambled up to a crouch. Careful to keep his head below the bushes surrounding the porch, he screamed for Ava to get behind the couch with Missy.

Gabe surged through the doorway onto the porch. "What's going—"

"Get down!" Jack yelled.

Gabe dropped instantly.

"Sniper." Jack pointed down the street in the direction the shot had come from. "He took a shot at Big Earl as he came through the door."

A shot that probably would have taken Jack out had he arrived in an official vehicle and a uniform, if Missy's statement was accurate. But why? What would make someone break into Ava's house and threaten to harm a random fireman? And then follow through on the threat. Or, at least, try. Unless the attacker intended to kill a specific fireman.

TWO

Ava hid behind the couch, covering Missy as best she could, though she was pretty sure Missy was safe for the moment. And probably for the next twenty-four hours, if her assailant had been honest. But who knew? Anyone who would kill just to make a point would probably not blink twice at lying. And she wasn't about to take any chances.

She was already risking enough by having the police there. Hopefully her attacker realized the nine-one-one call went through before he issued his demands and that she'd be smart enough to say as little as possible.

All of the blinds were closed, and the living room and foyer were a beehive of activity, with police officers and firefighters blocking any view Ava might have of the outdoors, though general consensus was he'd taken the shot and disappeared.

She peered over the back of the couch.

Her heart had stopped beating in the first few moments after Jack had tackled Big Earl, wondering if she'd have to live with either or both of their deaths on her conscience. But Jack had helped him to his feet, and they'd both spent the past few minutes answering questions. Surely if Earl had been seriously injured, he'd be on his way to the hospital instead of talking to the police.

Missy sobbed softly. "Is Big Earl okay?"

"Yes, honey." She kissed her head, the scent of her sweat-soaked hair grounding Ava in the midst of chaos. Missy was safe. Right now, that was all that mattered. But she'd have to make a decision soon. While the first officers to respond had taken a quick statement, they'd been more concerned with trying to apprehend the intruder and get Ava medical attention for her injuries than with why he'd broken in. That would now change. As it was, she'd kept what she told them to a minimum; someone had broken in, threatened her, threatened to kill a firefighter—she couldn't live with anyone being injured because she'd withheld that information, and that was all she knew. *God forgive me for not being completely honest.*

"What about Fireman Jack? Is he okay too?"

And please keep my baby safe.

"Yes, he's fine too." Ava lifted Missy awkwardly with her injured arm and rounded the back of the couch. She sat in the corner of the cream fabric sectional, where she could keep a close eye on whomever entered the front door, with Missy in her lap.

Missy laid her head against Ava's chest and popped her thumb in her mouth, a habit she'd broken more than a year ago.

"Oh, sweetie. No more tears, okay?" She stroked her hand over Missy's wild curls, gaining as much comfort as she offered. "Everything's going to be okay."

Her sniffles broke Ava's heart. To think she'd been

upset with Missy less than an hour ago for popping all the keys off her computer keyboard. She shook her head.

Oh, God. Please help me keep her safe. The silent prayer had been her constant companion over the past four years—ever since the day she found out she was pregnant.

When Liam had left the house that morning, he'd planned to talk to someone at the police station. He'd promised to tell Ava everything when he returned that evening. Even though she'd tried to question him, especially after he'd packed what he'd referred to as their flight bag—all of the things they'd need to go on the run at a moment's notice, if necessary—he hadn't been completely forthcoming. He'd said she'd be safer if she didn't know all the details, didn't know who he suspected was involved.

He was wrong.

And when she'd begged him to leave the investigating to the police, he'd adamantly refused. Who knew? Maybe someone had threatened him as they had her earlier tonight. He'd have done anything to keep Ava safe. Never mind the child they hadn't yet known about.

When the doctor had called a few hours later and confirmed the pregnancy she suspected, she'd been so excited. Everything else got pushed to the background at the thought of the child growing within her. Surely, once Liam told the police what was going on, they'd handle it, and all of Liam's fears would end.

She'd waited patiently for him to return home from the firehouse so she could share the exciting news. He was going to be so thrilled. She'd prepared his favorite dinner, along with a chocolate cake, which he couldn't resist. But she'd never gotten to tell him. He'd been taken from her on that very day, and he'd died without ever knowing about his child.

She couldn't help but wonder, as she had every day for the past four years, would it have made a difference? If she'd had the opportunity to share the news with him before he'd left for the police station, would he have fled with her that day? Would he have let his obsession with finding the arsonist go? Would he have lived?

Pain knifed through her heart, and she pressed her injured hand against her chest, desperately trying to keep her sobs from escaping and upsetting Missy any further. She rocked slowly back and forth with her little girl. *I'm so sorry, Liam. Sorry I never got to share Missy with you, and sorry I have apparently failed to keep her out of harm's way.*

"Ava?"

She jumped, startled by the deep voice, and wiped the tears that had escaped and rolled down her cheeks. "In here, Big Earl."

He peered around the corner of the archway. "Is it okay if I come in?"

Relief tore through her at the interruption. The last thing she needed right now were memories that would make her unable to function. "Of course."

"What happ—" Big Earl strode through the living room doorway and stopped short, taking in the scene with a quick glance. "Well, well, well. What has you so upset, little one?"

Missy grinned, bringing Ava a rush of joy. "Big Earl. A bad man hurt Mama."

"I heard about that." The giant of a man had the personality of a teddy bear. He rubbed a hand over his shiny, bald head. "But you know what? He can't hurt you or Mommy now, because I won't let him."

Missy launched herself from Ava's lap and into Big Earl's arms. The two had grown quite close, despite Ava holding Earl at arm's length. No doubt Earl had nothing to do with a fire that happened twelve hundred miles away four years ago, but the situation with Liam had left Ava not trusting anyone. Especially a firefighter. Even if he was her friend Serena's husband. She'd have kept Serena at a distance too, if she could have gotten away with it, but Serena was persistent.

If Ava came to care about too many people, they'd just be taken from her anyway, as Liam had, as her parents and brother had when she'd been only eighteen. Seemed everyone Ava let herself love was taken from her. She longed to have Missy back in her protective embrace.

"Fireman Jack said that too," Missy said.

"Fireman Jack, huh?" Big Earl laughed as he looked over Missy's shoulder to study Ava.

"Yup." She smiled and pointed at Jack as he walked in carrying two boxes Ava assumed held the supplies he'd need to treat her injuries.

Jack nodded on his way past.

"So, Jack…" Earl grinned and bounced Missy in his arms. "I see you've met our little Mischief."

Missy giggled at the nickname the firefighters had given her after Ava's first few 911 calls had brought them to rescue Missy from one childhood calamity or another. Thankfully, nothing too serious. Until tonight.

Jack's eyebrows drew together. "Mischief?"

"Let's just say this little one getting up to no good…"

He gestured toward Missy and laughed a deep, contagious belly laugh. "Isn't all that unusual."

"I'm sorry." Ava sniffed, desperately trying to get her out-of-control emotions under control.

"It's okay, Ava. Don't worry about anything." Taking advantage of Earl holding Missy, Jack squatted in front of Ava, set a box on the floor next to him and opened it. "Why don't you let me treat you now, though?"

Ava peered around him, keeping her gaze firmly on Missy.

Seeming to understand, Jack crouched lower so she could see past him.

"Thank you. I know she's fine, especially with Big Earl, it's just…" How could she explain the fear that gripped her anytime she thought her daughter might be in danger? Or the profound relief that assailed her when the perceived threat ended? Or the dreaded panic attacks that left her nearly incapacitated? She understood all of them, logically, but her emotions often got the best of her.

Jack awkwardly patted her hand. "Hey. It's perfectly normal to get upset when your child is frightened and crying."

He understands. That set off a new bevy of emotions, and tears threatened. *Oh, man. This is ridiculous.*

Missy popped her head up from Earl's shoulder just then, giving Ava the couple of seconds she needed to compose herself. "Hey, Big Earl. Did you bring the truck?"

"Well, hon, I didn't bring the big one this time, but I have the little one."

As if nothing had ever happened, Missy wiped her

face and bounced up and down in his arms. "Can I make the lights go? And the siren?"

"Sure can."

Missy turned to Ava. "Can I, Mama?"

Fear squeezed the breath from her lungs. Her first instinct was to say no. She wanted to lift Missy up and cradle her in her arms, cocoon her in safety.

Jack leaned close to her ear and whispered. "The police have secured the scene, so it's safe. And it's probably better for Missy if she's not here while they question you."

Of course, they'd question her. And Missy had already understood the threat to hurt a firefighter from the few initial questions that had been asked and answered. Since Ava hadn't yet decided how much to share with the police, though probably not everything given the threat her attacker had made toward Missy, Jack was right. It would be better to have Missy somewhere safe while she spoke with them.

"I'll open the blinds so you can see her the whole time." Jack left her to do so.

She had a perfect view of Big Earl's truck parked at the curb in front of the house. "Sure, baby, you can go with Big Earl, but only right to the truck and then straight back in, understand?"

"Got it." Missy's grin made her heart nearly burst. She waved at Jack. "Bye, Fireman Jack."

"See ya, Mischief." Jack cleaned Ava's head wound, applied several butterfly bandages and taped a gauze pad over her temple. Then he set to loosely wrapping her wrist. "I'll leave room to allow for further swelling, but you really should have this looked at."

"It'll be fine. I can always see my own doctor later

on." If she was still in town, which was highly doubtful. Even though the man had given her twenty-four hours, there was no way to know he'd been honest. Besides, even if he was, it wouldn't change the fact she didn't have what he wanted. Whatever flash drive he was looking for had probably disappeared with Liam, since she'd never come across anything like that.

She'd managed to escape once before. On the night her husband was killed, their home had been set ablaze, and she'd fled with nothing more than the flight bag he'd packed and a sniper taking shots. Thankfully, their many camping trips had given her the knowledge to head into the Florida wilderness behind their home and disappear. That, and the fact the sniper had anticipated she'd flee in her vehicle and positioned himself poorly had saved her.

Jack pinned the bandage in place, then stared her straight in the eye. "Will you actually go to the doctor?"

She shrugged. Though she didn't want to lie to him, she couldn't explain the full situation either. "Probably not, unless it gets worse."

"Miss Colburn?" Gabe approached, notebook in hand. "Mind if I ask a few questions?"

Yes, actually. Though he'd been kind enough to phrase it as a question, Ava had no illusions. He had every intention of asking her those questions.

"Of course. But could we make it kind of quick, please? I want to get Missy back to bed for a little while." Hints of morning light had already begun to peek over the horizon.

Jack stood, studying her closely, then apparently gave up his quest to change her mind. "I hope you feel better."

"Thank you." The thought of him leaving brought a

surprise rush of disappointment. For some reason, she'd felt protected with him at her side.

He smiled. "Anytime."

Jack's warm smile stirred something Ava hadn't felt in more than four years. Feelings of safety she refused to give in to or even acknowledge. Feelings she'd never experience again. Especially not for a fireman—even a fireman with a scruffy five-o'clock shadow, shaggy dark hair, and eyes the color of melted chocolate. Or any other man.

She'd already made her peace with God—sort of— and accepted what she'd never thought she could accept: the loss of her parents, the loss of her brother, the loss of the man she'd loved with all of her heart, but she'd promised herself she'd never go through it again. She had enough trouble just keeping Missy safe. And plenty of stress worrying over her.

She never should have settled down. Should have known better than to try. When she'd fled her home in rural Central Florida, she'd moved north through several states, including her longest stay in Rhode Island where it was legal to give birth to Missy in her run-down, one-room apartment with the assistance of a midwife. She'd eventually ended up in Seaport and rather than staying for a month or two then moving on to start over again somewhere new, wanting to give Missy a home, thinking she had to be safe from discovery after all that time, she'd gone to work for a florist six months ago and had begun to build a home for Missy.

When Marcy told her she was going to sell the shop and offered her the first chance at buying it, Ava had desperately wanted to say yes. But how could she buy a business when she was living under an assumed name, working for cash and might need to go on the run at a moment's notice? Easy. She couldn't.

She'd be better off buying an RV or something, moving them every few months.

"Well, I'd better be going." Jack backed toward the door.

Part of her wanted to ask him to stay. All the more reason to let him go. "Thank you, again."

"No problem." He lifted the first aid boxes.

"Goodbye, Jack." She watched him go, then let out the breath she'd been holding. Hopefully, and for more than one reason, that would be the last time she'd run into Fireman Jack.

Ava answered the officer's questions, without telling him about her husband or their connection to the arsonist in Florida. Liam's insistence they couldn't trust anyone had scared her even before she knew about Missy. No way she'd involve the police now that her child's life had been threatened. Especially after Liam was killed the very day he'd sought help from the police in Florida. The police wouldn't be able to help her, and if she involved them, her assailant might just decide to grab Missy sooner. Plus, it would just prolong the questioning. She needed them gone so she could try to escape while the coast might still be clear.

As soon as he walked out the door, she called Missy back in, said goodbye to Big Earl and locked the door behind him. She set Missy up in the living room, with a movie and the blinds tightly closed, then she grabbed the flight bag she still kept packed.

She ran her fingers over the blue duffel bag's zipper, wishing she'd been able to keep all of Liam's things inside, lost in memories of the first time he'd shown her the bag and explained its purpose. Would it really hurt to pull one of his shirts out of the closet and take it with her? Probably not, but she'd removed Liam's belongings because she needed room for Missy's things, and Liam had been adamant only the most important necessities were to go in the bag.

Ignoring the pang of regret, she stuffed the bag into Missy's oversized diaper bag, grabbed her purse and looked around one last time.

She'd come to love the cozy, two-story cottage. For the first time, it was not easy to walk out. Not surprising, really, considering six months was the longest she'd stayed in any one place over the past four years. A stupid mistake. She should have known better, should have kept with her routine of moving around every month or two. But it had gotten to be so much with a baby, and she'd wanted Missy to experience a true home. And she'd hoped four years and twelve hundred miles would be enough to keep them safe. She'd been wrong. And that mistake had almost cost both of them their lives.

She wanted to take everything with her, wanted to stay and embrace the illusion of safety she'd created, but she couldn't. If her attacker was watching, which she hoped he wasn't since the officers had searched the neighborhood and not found him, he'd realize she was going to flee. Ignoring everything else, Ava grabbed a couple of pictures Missy had drawn off the refrigerator and added them to the bag.

"How come you're taking those to work?" Missy stood in the doorway with her blankie clutched tightly against her cheek and her thumb in her mouth.

Ava forced a smile. "Because I love them. Now, come on."

She opened the garage door, so if her assailant was watching he'd see she was only carrying what she usually left the house with, only a little earlier than she usually headed out to work. Not completely unusual. No way to tell if he'd had her under surveillance or for how long, though she had to assume he'd been watching her. She'd have to make things look as routine as possible, since, unfortunately, this time, fleeing on foot through the woods wasn't an option.

She moved Missy to the car quickly, placing her body between Missy and anyone who might be lying in wait, then buckled her into the car seat, hopped in the car and backed out of the driveway. A quick glance in the rearview mirror showed nothing but an empty street as the sun rose over the quiet neighborhood she'd come to love.

A tear tipped over her lashes and tracked down her cheek. She wiped it away and turned the radio to a soft rock station, hoping Missy would be exhausted enough to fall asleep before she realized they were passing the shop. As she turned onto the road that would take her into town, a black SUV fell into place behind her.

She couldn't see the driver through the tinted windows. Did she dare take the chance and try to flee? Maybe she should wait until later in the day and try to escape unnoticed. If she left in broad daylight, would her attacker risk running her off the road? Or worse? What if he had put a tracking device on the car? Okay, she had to think. Had to calm down.

Tears sprang into her eyes. Pain raced through her arm. A dull ache throbbed at her temples, reverberating through her entire head. She glanced in the rearview mirror again. The SUV still hugged her bumper, way too close to be a neighbor heading off to work.

* * *

Jack searched his mother's kitchen for his keys. He was sure he'd left them hanging in the garage when he came in early this morning. Though everything else was in its place, including the flannel shirt he'd hung on the hook next to where his keys should be, the keys were nowhere to be found. He pulled open the cabinet beneath the sink. Cleaning supplies, sponges, paper towels—

"What are you looking for?"

Startled by his mother's voice, he spun around. "Hey, Mom. I thought you went to take a nap."

She shrugged.

He gave up the search and pulled out a chair from the table, then gestured for her to sit. "Are you feeling all right?"

She patted his cheek, a small tremor shaking her hand. "I'm fine, dear, just thirsty."

Keeping an eye on her, he tried to gauge her mood as he opened the refrigerator and pulled out a pitcher of lemonade.

"I said I'm okay, Jacky. Now stop fretting over me." A brief smile flickered across her face, bringing back memories of his childhood. "Were you looking for something?"

He shook off a touch of sadness. He clearly remembered hanging the keys up right before he shrugged out of his shirt. He set a glass in front of his mother and filled it. "I can't find my keys. I thought I left them on the hook in the garage, but they're not there."

She frowned.

"I'm sorry. Did you want something else?" He gestured toward the glass she ignored.

"What?" She shook her head. "Oh, no. Lemonade is perfect, thank you."

"Is something wrong?"

Her frown deepened, and she lowered her gaze to the glass. "I could have sworn…"

"Are you okay, Mom?"

She jerked back, banging into the table and splashing lemonade over the top of the glass. Her pale blue eyes lit with joy. "I remember. They're in the shed."

"The shed?" He hadn't even gone into the shed since he looked for the drill a few days ago. He promised his sister he'd childproof the house before she moved in, not only for her children, but to make things easier and safer for Mom as well.

"It's such a nice morning. I was going to take a drive."

Fear gripped his heart in an iron vise. He would have to remember not to leave the keys where she could find them again.

"Then I decided to do some gardening instead." She frowned again and waved her hand dismissively. "It doesn't matter. I remember leaving them there in the shed."

Oh, God, thank You for watching out for her. The sense of responsibility weighed heavily, as did the fear of failing the most important woman in the world to him. He forced a smile and dropped a kiss on her head. "Thanks, Mom."

"Sure, dear." She stood and started out of the kitchen, leaving her untouched lemonade on the table. "I'm going to rest for a while."

"I have to go to the firehouse, but Darcy is going to come sit with you." Fortunately, her friend Darcy was usually available to come sit with her at a moment's notice if he had to run out.

She nodded as she shuffled toward the doorway, shoulders slumped just a little. She'd taken to spending too much time in the house lately. Maybe getting dressed up and going out for a little while would help her feel better.

"Mom?"

She paused and turned back to him.

"After my shift, would you like to go to the church picnic?"

Her eyes brightened immediately. "That would be lovely, dear."

"Good. I'll see you in a little while, then." He turned away and headed out the door. Once he found the keys, which were exactly where his mother said she left them, he headed toward the firehouse. His mother had a doctor's appointment coming soon—an appointment Jack had every intention of attending with her. Hopefully, he'd get some answers then. She seemed so lucid sometimes. There had to be some kind of hope. He refused to accept there was nothing they could do to help her memory.

He slowed as he drove past Ava's house, quiet now, and wondered how she and Mischief were doing after their ordeal. The thought brought a smile as he tried to imagine what sort of trouble could have earned the adorable little girl the nickname that somehow seemed to suit her.

He hoped Big Earl had been able to talk Ava into seeking medical attention, though Jack doubted it. She seemed pretty adamant last night she would heal on her own.

He shook off the overwhelming concern, telling himself it was perfectly normal to worry about someone he treated. It wasn't like he was interested in the pretty woman with the big, blue eyes and the spunky personality, wasn't like he was going to stay in Seaport for more than the six months he'd promised his mother and sister.

When he ran up Ava's walkway last night, it was dark, and he'd been too concerned about who was injured to take much notice of his surroundings. As he stared at the stone walkway now, he couldn't help but notice the abundance of colorful flowers lining both sides of the path. Though he couldn't name most of them, the combination of colors worked to make the cozy little cottage welcoming. His mother used to keep flower beds out front. Now she couldn't remember to take care of them most days. Sadness intruded on the peace he'd found only a moment ago. Maybe he'd plant some flowers for her and tend to them while he was here. His sister would keep them up once she moved in.

A knock on his car window ripped him from his reverie.

He hadn't even realized he stopped in front of the house. "Can I help you, officer?"

"Are you stopped here for a reason?" Unlike Gabe the night before, this officer wasn't familiar to Jack.

"I'm sorry. I'm a firefighter, and I treated the woman who was injured here last night. I was just driving past on my way to work and got to wondering how she and her little girl were doing."

The young officer, a spattering of freckles across the bridge of his nose, smiled. "Since she headed out to work, I'd say she's feeling better."

Work? How could she work with that wrist? "Did you catch the intruder who hurt her?"

His expression sobered. "No, sir. Not yet. But we will."

Jack nodded. He thanked the officer and shook off his lingering daydreams and started driving, keeping his focus on the road ahead.

A sneaking suspicion that Ava knew more than she'd shared with the police seeped in. She'd been jumpy, understandable under the circumstances, but he'd seen something else in her eyes as well. Fear, yes. Pain. Concern for her daughter. But still something more. Resignation, maybe?

He took a deep breath in and let it out slowly. It shouldn't matter to him. *Didn't* matter. She was just a nice woman who might harbor some secrets she didn't wish to share, nothing more. Most likely nothing sinister.

So, why would whoever had broken into her house threaten to kill a firefighter? Why take a shot at Big Earl when he showed up? Was he the main target? Did the intruder know about her friendship with Earl? Had he targeted her while Earl was on duty hoping to draw him out?

So many questions swirled around in his head, the most pressing of which was why couldn't he get Ava out of his head when he couldn't possibly be anything to her?

He would never trust any woman again, but if he ever were to get involved with someone, it would definitely not be someone with a child. He'd married his ex-wife, despite her cheating on him and becoming pregnant when they were engaged, with forgiveness and a promise to raise the child as his own. He'd been so quick to forgive, so sure that had been God's plan for him.

And yet, two years later, after he completely fell in love with his little boy, Matthew, she'd walked out with him to marry the boy's father, leaving Jack with a horrible choice: try to maintain a relationship with the child, despite his mother's and father's wishes, or walk away from a child he'd grown to love. Since he'd only wanted what was best for Matthew, and his mother and father were treating him well, Jack walked away and left him to grow up in a good family. But he was left heartbroken and unable to trust anyone, even God.

No, there was zero chance he would ever get involved with another woman with a child and less than zero chance he'd get involved with anyone who was so clearly hiding something.

As he pulled into the parking lot, Big Earl was just walking out of the firehouse. Jack yelled to him as he got out. He needed to have a conversation with him, make sure he was careful until the police found Ava's attacker, just in case he was the target.

Big Earl stopped and waved. "I was just running across to the flower shop to check in on Ava and Mischief. Plus, I have to pick up flowers for Serena for our anniversary. Want to take a walk?"

He should say no. He should thank Big Earl but decline. He should go into the firehouse and spend some more time getting to know his coworkers, the people he'd be responsible for and who'd be responsible for him in the event of an emergency, at least, until he could get Big Earl alone for a few minutes to discuss his suspicions. "Sure, I'll take a walk."

"Seems Mischief took a liking to you." Earl clapped

him on the back. "You're good at what you do, man. You sure you don't want to stay in Seaport permanently? I know it's a volunteer fire department, but there are plenty of jobs around here, employers who understand when you have to run out."

Jack laughed. Earl had been asking him that since they'd met, which was only a few weeks ago, but Jack had worked too hard to get out of Seaport. He'd built a life for himself in New York City and had no intention of returning to the small town on Long Island permanently.

So he did what he always did when Earl asked; he changed the subject. "How long have you known Ava?"

"Since she moved here." He was quiet for a minute while they waited for the light to change. "About six months or so, I guess."

The fact she'd only been there for such a short time surprised Jack for some reason. "She's not married?"

Earl shot him a knowing look, and Jack squirmed.

Narrowing his eyes, Earl held his stare. "She's a nice girl, Jack."

He bristled. What was he trying to imply? "What's that supposed to mean? I was just asking."

So why did he feel so defensive?

"Look. My wife is friends with Ava. Good friends. Ava's…" Earl rubbed a hand over his bald head. He seemed to be searching for a word. Maybe some explanation as to why Ava's eyes were filled with so much distrust? "Fragile. It's not my place to share her story, at least, what I know of it, though I suspect there's more. But, either way, she's not the kind of woman you run out on in six months. Get what I'm sayin'?"

He did. And he was a little insulted. At first. But then

he saw the truth in the other man's eyes. He wasn't kidding. Ava must have been seriously hurt at some point.

Earl's expression softened, and he shook his head as they started across the street. "She's a sweetheart, and she's strong. Stronger than I think I could ever be. But she's had it tough, and that little girl of hers is a handful. She's got enough on her plate just getting through each day."

Big Earl stopped in front of the flower shop door and stared at the Closed sign.

"Is something wrong?" Jack stood beside him outside the flower shop.

He rubbed a hand over his head. "I don't know. It's not like Ava to be late."

A small niggle of worry crept in. "How long ago should she have been here?"

With a quick glance at his watch, Earl frowned. "About an hour ago."

"Do you want to call and check on her?"

A delivery van pulled up to the curb, and the driver jumped out. He studied a paper in his hand then looked up at the address. "Is the shop open?"

"Not yet."

He rounded the van and opened the back doors, then started pulling out large bins of flowers and lining them up on the sidewalk in front of the shop.

Earl's sigh of relief stole Jack's attention. "There she is."

Ava pulled her car against the curb behind the truck, jumped out and watched a black SUV roll past the small lot. Her hand shook violently as she tucked her hair behind her ear, turned to the truck driver and frowned.

The driver stopped when Ava started toward him. "Ma'am?"

Ava glanced over her shoulder at her car, then scanned the street before speaking. "What are you doing?"

"Making a delivery." He handed Ava a slip of pink paper.

Her jittery gestures set Jack's nerves on edge as well, and he found himself searching the empty street.

Ava's mouth fell open as she stared at the driver. "No. Wait. This is a mistake. I didn't order these."

He pointed to the page clutched in her hand. "That there says you did."

She shoved a hand into her hair and squeezed the strands. "Please, you have to take these back."

"Sorry, ma'am. I can't do that."

"Please. I…" Glancing behind her again, she huffed out a breath, turned and ran around to the passenger side of her car. She opened the back door and pulled Mischief out of the car seat then kept her in her arms as she returned to the driver. "Look, I didn't order…"

She stilled, her eyes widening, and she glanced at the little girl. "Oh, no, Missy, what did you do?"

"I'll need you to sign that, please." The driver once again pointed to the page he'd handed her.

Massaging her temples, Ava tried to reason with the driver. "Look. I had a rush order up on my computer, but I didn't submit it. My daughter must have accidentally hit the button. I have to cancel this. You have to take these back."

The driver shook his head, glancing at the paper in her hand. His eyes filled with regret. "I really am sorry, but I don't have the authority to do that. You'd have to call the company and work something out with them."

Her gaze left the driver and skimmed the lot, then landed on another black SUV with darkly tinted windows just pulling out from a side street and turning toward them.

Was it the same one from earlier? Jack tried to get a look at the tag, just in case it passed by again, but he couldn't make it out from where he stood.

She clutched her daughter tightly against her and turned her back to the street. "Can you wait while I try to reach them?"

The driver was shaking his head before she even finished asking the question.

"Big Earl." Mischief reached both hands toward him, swinging back and throwing Ava off balance.

Jack and Earl dove for Mischief at the same time.

Ava stumbled but caught her, then sighed and handed her to Earl. She threw her hands up, then took the pen from the driver, signed the paper and handed it back to him. After unlocking the door, she quickly ushered Big Earl inside with Mischief, then, without another word, she went to move her car.

Earl frowned after her.

"Do you think she's okay?" Jack squinted against the bright sunlight, keeping focused on Ava as she climbed from the car, locked it and headed back to them across the small lot, her head constantly swiveling from one side to the other the entire time.

"Fireman Jack." Mischief reached for him, and a small surge of happiness filled him as he took her from Earl.

"Hey, Mischief. How are you doing this morning?"

She wrapped her arms around him, squeezing his neck. "Hungry."

He laughed. "We'll have to get you something to eat, then."

She bounced up and down. "Chee-yos."

Ava opened the door and rushed back inside.

Jack put Mischief down beside Ava, then hurried out, grabbed a bin of flowers, and brought them back inside. "Where do you want these?"

She blew out a breath, blowing her hair up off her forehead, and rolled her eyes. "In the fridge, I guess."

When she started to reach for a bin, Jack held out a hand to stop her. "Big Earl and I will get them. How's your wrist?"

She held it up, moved her fingers, and winced. "I think it'll be okay."

"And your head?"

"I'm not gonna lie. I've had a killer headache all night. And this…" She gestured at all the flowers. "Isn't helping."

He and Earl continued to move the flowers. Jack tried to ignore Earl's constant scrutiny as he watched Ava.

She stopped in the middle of the room, her gaze on Mischief trying to help Earl wrestle a bin into the walk-in refrigerator. The tears in her eyes stopped just short of spilling over. If her red-rimmed, puffy eyes were any indication, she'd already shed her share of tears since he left her last night.

He couldn't help but wonder how much of what was bothering her she'd be willing to share. Not everything, of that he was certain. "Rough morning?"

Her shaky smile was like a punch to the gut. "You don't know the half of it."

He laughed, but tension still coiled at the base of his neck. Something was wrong. Her nerves were strung so tight it was a wonder she didn't snap. And somehow, he didn't think it was all over a mistaken flower order.

Ava pulled several flowers from the small refrigerator behind the counter and started putting together the bouquet Earl had come in for. She seemed to be managing okay with her injured wrist, though she did favor it. She glanced out the big front window. "What about you, Jack? I now have a ton of extra flowers I hate to see go to waste. Is there someone special you'd like flowers for?"

Flowers always brought his mother such happiness. "Actually, yes. My mom loves flowers."

She grabbed a few more sheets of tissue paper and started on a second bouquet, her gaze bouncing constantly from Mischief, to the street outside and back again. And it hit him. She wasn't acting like a woman who was upset over a rough morning. She was acting like a woman who was completely terrified. Had the intruder from the night before scared her that badly? He couldn't blame her if that was the case.

The ringing of his cell phone pulled him from any further contemplation. "Hello."

"Jack?"

"Yes? Darcy?" He should have looked at the caller ID before he answered, would have if his mind hadn't been preoccupied with such unsettling thoughts.

"Everything's okay, but your mother's in the emergency room. I'm sorry. I only turned my back for a minute."

"I'm on my way." He disconnected and shoved the phone in his pocket. "I'm sorry. I have to run."

Was that disappointment in Ava's eyes or was that wishful thinking?

"Here." She held the bouquet out to him. "Don't forget your flowers."

Urgency beat at him as he reached for his wallet. "How much?"

She held up a hand. "Nothing. They're a thank-you for helping us last night."

Normally, he would have insisted on paying, but fear for his mother wouldn't allow the delay, so he simply thanked her and ran out the door, barely checking for oncoming traffic as he crossed the road to reach his car. He climbed in and tossed the flowers onto the passenger seat. Though he was tempted to attach his emergency light, he didn't. While he couldn't deny the urgency of the situation, this was personal.

As he raced toward the hospital on streets that were as familiar to him as if he'd never left, he still couldn't wrap his mind around the fact that he was back in Seaport. He'd spent his entire childhood and teenage years waiting for the day he could leave Seaport for the big city, when he could become a fireman and honor his father's memory.

He loved the constant motion of New York City, no matter the time of day or night, and being able to find somewhere open for breakfast when he left work at two or three in the morning. He embraced the anonymity. If Carrie had left him in Seaport, the entire town would have known what happened and spent the rest of his life staring at him and clucking their tongues with sympathy every time he turned his back.

And now, none of that mattered. All that mattered was getting to his mother and making sure she was safe. He slammed on his brakes for a red light and reached out a hand to stop the flowers from flying off the seat. And Ava mattered. She'd piqued his curiosity. He wasn't sure what was going on with her, but he would like the opportunity to find out what she was hiding. For now, he had to handle one crisis at a time.

He whipped into the hospital parking lot, threw his car into Park and jumped out, then jogged across the lot and strode through the emergency room doors. Thankfully, it wasn't crowded, and he spotted his mother's friend right away. "What happened?"

"I'm so sorry. I already called your sister. She's on her way."

A stab of guilt hit him. He should have called her, but he'd been so worried—and preoccupied—he hadn't thought of it.

Darcy continued, "I didn't even realize she'd turned the stove on. It must have been on for a while, but she went into the kitchen for a drink. I was right behind her."

Jack prayed for patience. Understanding she was rambling because she was upset didn't make the wait any easier.

"And she burned her hand."

"How bad?"

"Not that bad. I think she was more upset than anything. She's right through there. They said to send you in when you got here."

He started toward the doors then paused. "Thank you, Darcy."

The older woman's shoulders slumped as if a weight had been lifted.

As soon as he entered the emergency room, he saw his mother sitting on a stretcher, her legs dangling over the side. *Thank You, God.* He gripped her uninjured hand and brought it to his lips. "Are you all right?"

Tears shimmered in her eyes, tearing a hole in his heart. "I'm sorry, Jacky."

Relief battered him, softening some of the frustration. "Don't be silly, Mom. It was an accident. As long as you're okay…"

"I'm fine." She held up her bandaged hand. "It wasn't very bad, and they gave me something for the pain."

Keeping her hand in his, he studied her.

She shook her head, lowering her gaze to the injured hand now resting in her lap. Her eyebrows drew together, her voice no more than a raspy whisper. "I don't know what happened. No matter how hard I try, I just can't remember turning the stove on."

"It's all right, Mom."

The tears spilled over, running down her cheeks.

Jack resisted the urge to rub his chest. It wouldn't ease the ache there anyway. "It'll be okay, Mom."

"No. It won't." Soft sobs shook her frail shoulders. His mother had always been a petite woman, but she'd never seemed fragile. Until now. "I can't remember what happened."

He slid onto the stretcher and turned to face her. "I promise, Mom. We'll work this out. Trust me."

"I do, Jacky."

He pressed his forehead to hers. "I'll take care of you."

He asked for her trust, but truthfully, he didn't have a clue what he was going to do. He'd moved out here to take care of her, but he couldn't be with her every minute, and they had a good support system in place. He sighed and pulled his mother closer. Somehow, they'd make it work. His mother had managed to take care of him and his sister after their father, who was also a firefighter, had been killed in the line of duty when they were young, and that couldn't have been easy either. She'd always sworn her faith had seen her through the darkest times.

Jack's faith had always been strong, though it had wavered after his wife left him. He'd done everything he could, ignored his own pain and offered her forgiveness, tried to follow the path he thought God had laid out for him. He'd tried to get her to attend counseling with him, tried desperately to save their marriage—a marriage that had been doomed from the start—but she made it clear she'd already moved on. And he'd had no choice but to let go of her and Matthew. And his faith had faltered.

Crushed, he'd prayed for strength and guidance, his waning faith only adding to the pain of losing his family. And now God expected him to watch his mother slowly fading away. Surely, He'd offer guidance, provide some way to save her if only Jack could understand what he was supposed to do.

"I love you, Jacky."

He stood and wrapped his arms around her, lowering his chin into her thinning blue curls. He forced aside his worries for the future and squeezed his eyes closed against the tears he wouldn't shed in front of her. "I love you, Mom."

She hugged him, then sat back, looking so lost.

He took her delicate hand in his, rubbing his thumb

over the paper-thin skin. He smiled through the anguish. "Come on. Let's see if they'll let you go home soon. I brought you a present."

His mom lifted her head, the smile shining in her eyes. "Really?"

"Yup." He thought of the bouquet on his front seat and sent a silent thank-you to Ava. He'd have to remember to stop in and tell her how special her gesture had been. And then he'd walk away. Curious or not, Ava was one complication he couldn't handle right now.

THREE

Ava moved a small vase into the front window, re-arranging the flowers as she scanned the street and searched the firehouse parking lot. The irony of working across the street from a firehouse hadn't been lost on her when she'd seen the Help Wanted sign in the window, but the cozy little shop had seemed so welcoming.

Though she'd tried to lose her tail on the way to the shop—stopping to run imaginary errands, get gas, circle the long way around to the shop—she hadn't been able to shake him, so she'd been forced to go to the shop and rethink her options. And since she arrived at the shop, she'd seen the black SUV stopped at the traffic light out front several times, had seen it at the gas station down the road, even in the firehouse parking lot for a minute, until she moved closer to the window and he took off. If he'd settle on one surveillance spot, she might be able to slip out either the front or back door undetected. As it was, he kept circling, cutting off any means of escape.

She'd already racked her brain, trying to think of who she could call for help, who Liam might have left whatever evidence he had with, where he might have hidden a flash drive, but she was no closer to solving the mystery now than she had been last night. Obviously, whoever Liam had trusted had betrayed him. Or the police had. So that left her nowhere.

And time was running out. The constant *tick, tick, tick* of the clock in her head threatened to drive her mad.

She tried praying, but no revelations came. Instead, her prayers turned into a constant mantra: *please, keep Missy safe, please, keep Missy safe...*

What she needed was a plan, some way to get out of there without her stalker seeing her. But in a town the size of Seaport, disappearing discreetly wasn't that easy.

Ava rolled up the napkins from Missy's lunch, then winced at the pain in her wrist. If she were honest, it hurt worse than she'd let on when Jack asked. Jack: a distraction she most definitely did not need. If God had meant for her to be with someone, He wouldn't have taken Liam.

She tossed the napkins on top of her paper plate then threw everything in the trash. A glance at Missy sitting cross-legged on a mat on the floor, happily squishing Play-Doh creations, told her she'd probably have a few minutes of quiet. She lifted the receiver and dialed Mrs. Worthington's number again. Still busy. *Ugh...* She was going to have to do something with all of these flowers. She didn't have it in her to leave them all to die, but she wanted to double-check that the party was canceled. With the Worthingtons, you never knew. It wouldn't be the first time they'd canceled an order then changed their minds.

She blew out a breath and rubbed her temples. Who was she kidding?

Truth was, no matter how much she'd come to love

Seaport, she couldn't ignore the threat to Missy. They had to get out of there, had to start over on a path of moving from one town to the next, never settling, never putting down roots, making friends, or embracing a community. Obviously, that wasn't the path she was supposed to follow. So, now, she just had to figure out how to get out of there unseen.

The bell above the door chimed, signaling a customer, and she jumped. Her gaze shot to the woman who entered, and she forced a smile. "Hi, Serena. What are you doing here?"

"Please, girl, did you really think I wouldn't stop in to check on you after Big Earl told me what happened?" Serena was in her early fifties, but she didn't look a day over thirty with her high cheekbones, flawless, tan skin, and long blond hair she usually wore pulled back in an elaborate braid. She was a remarkable woman. In more ways than one. Not only did she work, keep house and raise four children, she was also quite active in the community and the church. She attributed her good fortune to hardy genes and a loving family. Ava didn't know if it was true, but whatever it was, she was an admirable woman and a wonderful role model. She was also the first real friend Ava had made upon moving to Seaport.

And now she had to get rid of her. "Thanks, Serena, but I'm fine, really."

Serena peered at her from the corners of her eyes and lifted a brow.

"Seriously." She forced a smile and begged forgiveness for the lie meant to keep Serena from looking too deeply into her past so she'd be safe.

"Rena." Missy ran to Serena and threw her arms around her legs.

"Hey, sugar." She lifted Missy. "You sure are getting big. What's your mama been feeding you?"

Missy's giggles echoed through the shop. "Peanut butter."

"Peanut butter, huh?" Serena set Missy down and rummaged through her bag and pulled out a Ziploc bag filled with homemade cookies. "Well, since you've already had your lunch, I guess it would be okay for you to have some of these."

"Yay." Missy clapped and took the bag. "I want one."

"Ahem." Ava waited for Missy to look up at her then lifted a brow.

"Oh. Uh." She grinned. "Thank you, Rena."

Serena grinned back at her and ruffled her curls. "You're welcome, and if it's all right with Mom, I'll set them up at the table for you with some milk."

"Go ahead, and I'll make tea." Ava filled mugs with water and popped them in the microwave while Serena helped Missy set out a dish and arrange the cookies. Since she couldn't safely flee yet, she would take this moment for herself, this one last instant of normalcy, of sharing with probably the last friend she'd ever make, since the rest of her life would be spent on the run. It would be safer to keep people at a distance. Besides, the people she came to care for usually ended up...

"I heard you had a bit of an adventure yesterday." Though Serena addressed the comment to Missy, she glanced over her head at Ava, eyebrows raised in a silent question.

Ava nodded, acknowledging Serena's concern and letting her know it was all right if Missy wanted to talk about it.

"Yup. And Big Earl let me play the sirens."

The microwave dinged, signaling the water was ready, and Ava dropped in a couple of tea bags. When she turned, Serena was standing beside her.

"Are you sure you're okay? Earl said you seemed stressed." She took one of the mugs from Ava but made no move to return to the table where Missy sat happily crunching cookies. Instead, she pitched her voice low. "You know, if you need anything, even a few hours to yourself, you just have to say the word."

Ava did know, and she appreciated it more than the other woman would ever know. "I know. Thanks, Serena."

Serena spent a lot of time at the firehouse, often bringing meals and treats to the guys. She and Ava had met when Ava first arrived in town, and Serena had stopped in for some flowers to make the place more cheerful. They'd developed an almost instant friendship, despite Ava's reluctance to get involved. When it came to people she cared about, Serena didn't take no for an answer.

Ava had no doubt she could talk to Serena about anything, but how did you explain something you didn't fully understand yourself? "I'm okay, I just have a lot on my mind. I know it's probably foolish, but sometimes I just feel so angry. And other times I just feel sad."

That was true enough, though certainly not the whole story.

Concern etched the lines furrowing Serena's brow. "That's perfectly normal, honey."

"Is it? Even after so many years? Don't get me wrong. It's not like I'm unhappy. I like my life here... love it really. I have friends, a job I enjoy, my home and a little girl that means everything in the world to me, and yet sometimes, I just feel like something's…" She shrugged, unable to explain the empty feeling in her gut, especially since she couldn't share the entire truth of her situation. "Missing."

"If that's what you feel, then something probably is. You just need to figure out what." Serena patted her hand. "Follow your heart, honey. It usually leads you where you need to be."

Ava laughed. "If only things were as easy as you always make them sound."

"Oh, they are, dear. Really. I learned that lesson a long time ago. It's called faith." She sipped her tea and glanced at Missy. "See, all you need to do is fill her belly and she drifts right off."

Missy still sat, arms folded on the table, head resting on her arms. Her mouth hung slightly agape, her soft breaths blowing up little puffs of cookie crumbs from the table.

Unable to resist, Ava set her mug on the counter, pulled out her cell phone and snapped a picture, a memory of the life she'd hoped to have. "She didn't sleep well last night."

She stuffed the phone in her pocket, lifted Missy and laid her on the couch in the back. "Speaking of last night, Mrs. Worthington canceled Cara's party. Again. Unfortunately, Missy hit Submit on the order, and now I'm stuck with all the flowers. Are you going to be at the hospital this afternoon?"

"Sure, why?"

After double-checking the back door had both locks engaged, for the hundredth time that day, she left Missy asleep with the door between the shop and the back room cracked open so she could keep an eye on her.

An idea had begun to form. There might only be two exits from her shop and her home, but the hospital had a dozen or more. It would mean they had to go on the run without her car, but she couldn't solve every problem at once. Right now, she needed to concentrate on getting away. Besides, they could well have planted a bug on her car while it had been sitting out in the lot. "I don't want all of these flowers to go to waste, so I thought I'd make up bouquets and take them over to the hospital later."

Serena studied her. "That would be amazing, but what if Mrs. Worthington decides the party's back on?"

"She won't. She was pretty adamant it was off." And even if she did, it would be too late. Ava would already be gone.

"Surely, you're not going to give all of them away?" She lifted a skeptical brow. "You could probably sell some, especially if you discount them."

Ava had forgotten for a moment how perceptive Serena was. A mistake she'd need to be careful not to repeat. She offered a smile. "I'm not going to give away all of them, just some. I'll never sell them all before they die."

Her expression softened. "That would be so sweet. I'll be there, so just come by whenever you're ready."

"Thanks. Now, did you stop in for anything special this morning, or just to check up on us?"

Serena eyed her for another moment then smiled. "I'm making that man of mine a special dinner for our anniversary tomorrow night, and I wanted a little something pretty for the table. Kiara is taking Little Earl to the movies so Mom and Dad can have a peaceful dinner. That's one of the benefits of having kids with a big age gap, built in babysitter. Then we're all going to have family movie night. With popcorn, and I get to pick the movie for a change."

"It's about time." Ava sighed, relieved Serena didn't push for answers, even though Missy had fallen asleep and they could speak freely. "Do you know what you're looking for?"

"I thought maybe something with a couple of candles?" Serena leaned her elbows on the counter and propped her chin in her hands, watching Ava gather what she needed to start the centerpieces.

She'd make them something special, a thank-you for her friendship, an apology for not being able to say goodbye.

"So, I heard you met Jack."

Ava's hands stilled. Heat crept up her cheeks. "Oh?"

Serena's musical laughter danced over her. "He's a cutie. If I was twenty years younger and not already married to the sweetest man in the world, I might give you a run for your money."

And if I was not about to run in fear for my life, I may have someday given him a chance. But probably not. After all, no matter Ava's situation, Jack was still a firefighter. A firefighter with a sweet disposition and a killer smile. Though she'd made her peace with God—mostly—she wouldn't ever allow herself to have feelings for another man. Especially a man who worked in the same dangerous profession her husband had, a profession that got him killed, possibly by another firefighter. The same man who was now after her and Missy. Odd, her attacker happened to show up in town the same time as Fireman Jack.

Ava shot her best scowl at her friend, but she couldn't

help the laugh that bubbled out and ruined it as she continued to work. "Oh, stop yourself. I already told you, no more men for me."

Ava put the finishing touches on the arrangements, then wrapped them in cellophane.

"They're beautiful. Thank you so much." Dropping money on the counter, Serena lifted the two centerpieces and gave Ava a knowing look. "And as far as Fireman Jack goes, we'll see."

Ava said goodbye and held the door for her. Serena was a wonderful friend and a great person, but everything in her life was about family. The thought of not having her husband was so foreign to her, she couldn't understand how Ava wouldn't want to get married again, even though she knew Liam had been killed in the line of duty. But if she'd known him, known how good they were together, if Ava had been able to talk about him, about her parents, about her little brother, and the pain of losing so many of those she loved, she might understand.

The black SUV just turning the corner and heading away from the shop was a stark reminder that Ava couldn't have that, even if it was what she wanted. The thought of grabbing Missy up and running for the car almost propelled her into action, but a few deep breaths calmed her. The last thing she needed was to run into him in the parking lot. Better to stick to her plan. She turned, then stopped short. Fearing he'd change his mind about cruising the neighborhood hoping to intimidate her and come into the shop, she debated locking the door and turning over the Closed sign. But she needed to keep things as normal as possible. Closing the shop would only raise suspicion.

Ava started to clean up, washing Serena's mug and

putting it and the leftover cookies away. After sealing the bag, she contemplated it for a moment. Serena was also a fabulous baker. She worked early mornings at the local bakery. Ava opened the bag and pulled out a chocolate chip cookie. *Can't hurt to have just one.*

Three cookies and another mug of peach dream tea later, Ava brushed the crumbs from her hands, cleaned up and spread a blanket over Missy. She'd surely regret this nap later, but for now, she needed to put the quiet time to use. Smoothing Missy's curls back from her face, she tucked the blanket tighter and went out to the front.

With a sigh and one eye on the door, she started laying out sheets of cellophane along the table near the back of the shop. She spread a few pieces of fern on each piece then added some flowers. With the creativity came peace. She loved this part of her work. She pulled some hibiscus—orange and yellow—from a bin and added them to one of the bouquets. Orchids went into another. A colorful array of carnations with baby's breath. The joy of creating something that would bring someone happiness relaxed her. She rolled her shoulders and tilted her head from side to side before wrapping up the bouquets and stacking them in a box at the far corner of the table.

When she was done, she kept Missy with her as she loaded the flowers into the car, careful to appear as if this was part of her routine. If the man who'd accosted her was telling the truth, her volunteer work at the hospital, the volunteer work she'd started doing to appease some of her guilt for not trying to find out who'd killed her husband, had led him to her. Though she'd have done anything to find Liam's killer if she hadn't been pregnant, she had no doubt her husband would have expected her to protect his child over seeing his killer brought to justice, but the choice still didn't always sit well. Especially if it came at the cost of any more lives.

But what was she supposed to do? How could she trust the police when Liam had gone to them on the day he died? He didn't trust them, but in the end, he did what he thought was right. How was she to know that decision hadn't cost him his life? It didn't matter anyway. Even if she wanted to trust the police here, her assailant had been very clear, no police.

She locked up the shop midafternoon, not unusual if she was making a delivery, her gaze lingering one last time on what she was leaving behind: the opportunity to buy a business she loved and settle in a wonderful community. Then she turned away and strapped Missy into the car seat.

The SUV popped up in her rearview mirror as soon as she pulled onto the road.

Ava strode through the hospital corridor with a large box filled with bouquets and Missy at her side. She'd barely slept a wink last night. How could she even contemplate going on the run with a three-year-old and no vehicle?

Missy skipped along happily, curls bouncing, two bouquets clutched tightly against her chest. She glanced up and found Ava watching her, and a wide grin spread across her face, lighting her eyes.

Ava calmed instantly. She shrugged the diaper bag with the flight bag tucked inside higher onto her shoulder.

"Hi, Missy." Serena strode toward them.

"Rena." Missy ran to her, gripping one bouquet in each hand, and flung her arms around Serena's legs.

"What are you up to?" Serena laughed.

"We brought flowers." She held one pudgy fist out to Serena.

"Oh, thank you."

"And this one's for the sick people." Missy grinned, and pride lit her eyes as she held up the other crushed bouquet, two carnations dangling over the side of the cellophane from broken stems.

Ava found such joy in the fact Missy loved helping people. She had a special gift for making people feel good and left a trail of smiles in her wake no matter where she went.

"I'll bet Mr. Jenkins would love that one." Serena took Missy's free hand and started down the hallway.

Ava fell into step beside her. Sweat trickled down the sides of her face. When she'd asked if Serena would be at the hospital, she'd been hoping the other woman would say no. Escaping would be easier if Serena wasn't there. But she had no choice; her twenty-four hours was fast running out.

Serena gestured toward a partially open door on the right.

Ava peeked into the room where an elderly man lay staring at the ceiling. "What's Mr. Jenkins here for?"

"He fell and broke his hip again, that poor man."

"When is he going to stop being so stubborn and give in and use the walker?"

Serena shrugged. "Who knows?"

Ava knocked twice then pushed the door the rest of the way open and walked in.

"Hi, Mr. Jenkins," Serena yelled, since his hearing aids were sitting on the tray beside his bed. "Look, you have a visitor, and she brought flowers."

"Hi." Missy ran across the room and thrust the flowers toward Mr. Jenkins.

"Well, thank you. Aren't you a sweetheart?" He brought the bouquet to his nose and inhaled deeply. "Nothing like flowers to perk a man up."

Ava put the box down on the counter, took the bouquet from him and filled a cup with water. It almost slipped from her grasp, but she fumbled and caught it. She was going to miss this. "How are you feeling?"

"Eh, been better, been worse." He waved off her concern with a frail hand.

She put the flowers in the makeshift vase, breaking the bottom half of the stems off the broken ones and tucking what remained into the water. "Where's Mrs. Jenkins today?"

His eyes lit with the smile that curved his mouth. "I made her go home and rest for a little while. Been married sixty-five years, now, and that woman has never left my side."

"You're quite blessed."

"Yes, I am." He shot her a mischievous grin. "But then again, Mrs. Jenkins is blessed too."

"Yes, she is." Ava laughed. What would it be like to have someone to share your life with for sixty-five years? She tamped down the longing. Thoughts like that would only lead to heartbreak. She put the flowers on the nightstand and fussed with them for another minute, needing the time to collect herself.

"She promised she'd bring back some of her tuna casserole later on." He shook his head and laughed. "You'd think after sixty-five years, I'd have found a way to tell her I can't stand tuna casserole. Never could."

A genuine smile touched Ava. Mrs. Jenkins really

was blessed. "Come on, Missy. We still have a lot of flowers to deliver."

She handed Missy another bouquet, hefted the box up and waved to Mr. Jenkins. "Feel better, Mr. Jenkins."

"Thank you. And thank you for the flowers, young lady."

Missy beamed. "You welcome."

Serena walked beside Ava. "She's getting so big."

Missy danced in the middle of the hallway to some imagined tune only she could hear, holding up the bouquet of lilies, spinning around, ending with a curtsy.

"I know." Though every new experience, every phase and every moment with Missy thrilled her, Ava couldn't help being a little sad she was growing up so quickly.

She knocked twice before pushing open the next door. "Mrs. Romano?"

"Come in, dear."

"Look who came to see you."

Missy darted into the room, flowers held high. "Hi."

"Hello, little one. Are those for me?"

"Uh-huh."

"Well, aren't you sweet. Thank you. They're beautiful. Did you come to read with me today?"

Missy shot a hopeful glance at Ava.

Tick, tock, tick, tock. Sweat pooled at the base of her spine as she glanced at the clock. Run now, or give it a little longer? What would her attacker expect? "Sure, honey. We have time for a story."

"Yay." Missy clapped her hands together, wildly waving the bouquet as she did. "Can we read *Pooh*?"

"*Winnie the Pooh* it is." Mrs. Romano propped the back of the bed up higher and slid over a little.

Serena lifted Missy onto the bed beside the older woman and handed her the book from the nightstand.

Ava and Missy often visited Mrs. Romano and a few of the other patients from church when they were in the hospital. Mostly elderly patients whose families didn't live nearby or weren't able to visit often for some reason. Unfortunately, Mrs. Romano was battling cancer and spent a lot of time in the hospital. Her son lived in Georgia but came up at least one weekend a month, and volunteers from the church helped the rest of the time.

While Mrs. Romano read to Missy, Ava busied herself with the flowers.

Serena's cell phone chimed and she excused herself and ducked out of the room.

Hopefully, it would be something to drag her away so Ava could make her escape. She needed to get out of there soon, without stopping to answer questions.

"Oh, dear."

Pulled from her introspection by Mrs. Romano's small cry of alarm, Ava whirled toward the bed.

The bottom of the bed rose higher and higher, pushing Mrs. Romano's legs up.

"Oh, no." Ava searched frantically for the remote. She pulled Missy up, yanked back the covers, and sure enough, it was wedged beneath her. She pulled it out and pressed the button to lower her legs. "I'm sorry, Mrs. Romano. Are you all right?"

"I'm fine. I was just afraid Missy would fall off." She laughed as she pressed a hand to her chest and leaned back. "Ready to finish?"

Missy frowned and nodded. "Sorry."

"No worries, dear. Everything is fine." She set the

book back in her lap and pointed to the picture. "Now, let's see what Pooh and Piglet are up to."

Serena came back into the room. "Sorry, guys, but I have to run. Duty calls."

Ava kissed her cheek and resisted the urge to hug her tightly and say goodbye. No sense pinging her radar. With four kids, one of whom had been as big a handful as Missy growing up, Serena could sense trouble a mile away. As much as she wished she could confide in Serena, to share some of the burden of her past, she couldn't. All Serena knew was that her husband was a firefighter who'd been killed in the line of duty. Any more knowledge than that might put her in danger, even if Ava did want to tell her the truth.

Ava bit back tears as she watched Serena walk away. "Come on, Missy, it's time for us to get going too."

She said goodbye to Mrs. Romano and wished her well. Now for the hard part. She'd googled a satellite image of the hospital while Missy had slept earlier, and she was confident she could find her way to a side entrance that led to a small courtyard behind the parking lot. From there, they'd have to climb over a low stone wall, cross the highway and cut through the back of an abandoned gas station. All without drawing attention to herself and Missy. And if they could make it that far, there was a bus station one block over.

She'd left the box of flowers in Mrs. Romano's room, taking only the diaper bag with Liam's flight bag inside it. She clutched Missy's hand tightly, praying she wouldn't slip away or cause a fuss in the hospital. "I have a fun idea."

Missy frowned and looked around as they hurried

down a stairwell at the back of the hospital. "I wanna push the buttons."

"We can't take the elevator this time, honey. Maybe next time."

"But I like pushing the buttons."

"You can push the buttons later. For now, how'd you like to go on an adventure?"

Missy perked right up. "Yay."

When they reached the bottom of the stairwell, Ava paused. She sucked in a few deep breaths, searched for calm, prayed she was doing the right thing and shoved open the door. She poked her head out and looked around. No one nearby. "See that wall over there?"

Missy nodded.

"We're going to climb over that, okay?"

"But you always tell me don't climb on walls."

She counted to ten in her head as they crossed the courtyard. "I know, but this is different because it's part of the game. Okay?"

"Uhh…"

They reached the wall. Almost home free. She dropped Missy to the other side and kept a firm grip on her hand as she climbed after her. All that was left was to cross the street and disappear behind the gas station. So close.

She scooped Missy into her arms and fought the urge to run. Almost there. She looked both ways down the deserted street and started across.

The black SUV fishtailed around the corner and skidded to an abrupt stop, blocking her way. He must have been circling the hospital since she went in. She should have thought of that.

A man jumped out of the driver's side, pulling a ski mask down over his face.

Ava ran. She'd never make it back to the hospital, but if she could make it to the woods, she could disappear. But the bulky diaper bag swinging against her and Missy in her arms slowed her down.

The man tackled her to the ground.

She shielded Missy's head as she fell, contorting to keep from landing on her, and instead landed hard on her elbow and shoulder. Pain tore through her, even though the diaper bag cushioned some of her fall.

The man stumbled over her but regained his footing and grabbed Missy's arm. He kicked Ava and yanked Missy out of her embrace. "Maybe now you'll take me more seriously."

"No, please. I'm telling you I don't have what you're looking for."

The same cold eyes from the night before pinned her from beneath the black ski mask.

"Then I suggest you find out who does." He tucked Missy under his arm, turned and fled toward the car.

"No!" Ava lurched to her feet and ran after him. She'd chosen this spot to run because of its isolation, but surely someone would pass by if she could just hold him off.

"Mama!" Missy screamed and reached for her.

The man stopped to open the back passenger side door, and Ava plowed into him.

He backhanded her and shoved her aside.

She hit the car, rebounded and landed a solid kick to the side of his knee.

He went down, his hold on Missy loosening.

Missy squirmed away and ran.

Oh, please, God, don't let her run into the street. Please don't let her stay here, because I can't fight him off alone. Please, help me.

The man circled an arm around Ava's neck, pressed his other hand against the back of her head. His hold tightened, cutting off her airway, blocking her from screaming for help.

Blackness encroached, tunneling her vision. She clawed at his arm, searched for Missy and found her sitting on the side of the road sobbing. She tried to call out but couldn't past the arm blocking her throat. *Oh, baby, run. Please run.*

"Mama! Mama!" Missy's screams pursued her toward oblivion.

Jack unlocked the car door in the hospital parking lot and held it open for his mother.

"Thank you, dear." She took her time climbing into the car, and he wondered if she'd been injured worse than he'd thought.

"Are you okay?"

She paused halfway into the car, cocked her head to the side. "Do you hear that?"

"Hear what?"

She straightened and pointed toward the back of the parking lot just as the child's screams reached him.

"You stay right there, Mom. Please." He pocketed the keys, praying she'd stay where she was, and ran toward the screams. When he reached the back corner of the parking lot, he hopped the chain-link fence and crossed a small courtyard.

The child's screams intensified.

He hurdled a low stone wall at full speed. The instant he rounded a row of hedges bordering the road, the little girl came into view. She sat on the side of the road, sobbing and screaming for her mother. "Missy!"

She paused a moment, turned her attention to him and started to cry harder.

But Jack's attention had already turned to the man choking Ava. Wild rage tore through him as he ran toward them.

The man looked up, saw Jack coming, and loosened his hold from around Ava's neck.

Jack never even slowed down. With the full force of his weight, propelled by his speed, he plowed a fist into the attacker's jaw.

The man released his grip and staggered back against the car.

Ava's knees collapsed, and Jack caught her as she fell, still watching the man who'd attacked her.

The man's foot connected with Jack's stomach before he could block it, forcing him to double over as he tried to keep Ava from smacking her head against the ground.

Before he could straighten, the man slid over the hood of the SUV and jumped in. The tires spun, kicking up chunks of dirt and grass as he hit the gas.

Jack shoved Ava aside, a lot less gently than he'd have liked, and dove for Missy. He scooped her up and tumbled into a narrow drainage ditch with her cradled in his arms just as the SUV lurched forward toward her.

"Are you hurt, Missy?" Keeping a tight hold on her, Jack shot to his feet and started after the retreating vehicle. Mud smeared across the license plate covered the numbers, so he couldn't get anything, but there was no mistaking the colors of the Florida plate.

"Mama! Mama!" Missy screamed over and over.

Jack stopped short. This was foolish. He couldn't catch the man on foot. Missy was distraught and possibly injured, Ava was most definitely injured and in need of medical attention, and he could only pray his mother had stayed put when he'd asked her to. He had to let the attacker go.

He took a deep breath and struggled to rein in his anger. He would be of no help to anyone in his current condition. Panting hard, he prayed for patience, for the strength to take care of those who needed him and, perhaps selfishly, for the opportunity to come up against whomever had done this at another moment, when he would be more capable of defending those in need of protection.

"All right. Okay." He shifted Missy so he could look into her eyes, desperate to get to Ava, but knowing her first concern would be for her daughter. "Missy, honey, are you hurt? Mischief?"

"Mama!"

He smoothed her curls back out of her face and looked into her eyes. Pupils looked good, no visible signs of injury. "I know, baby. I'm going to help your mama, but I need to know if you're hurt first."

She looked into his eyes for the first time and frowned. "Fireman Jack?"

"Yes, honey, it's me. It's Fireman Jack."

She sniffed, and her sobs tapered off. He held out her arm and rubbed it. "The bad man pulled my arm."

No swelling, no bruising, but a red handprint circled her forearm where the man must have grabbed her. The anger surged again, a blazing inferno of rage. "Okay, we can fix that. Did you hit your head at all?"

She shook her head, her blond curls bouncing back into her eyes.

"All right, we're going to check on Mama now, okay? You stay right next to me." He crouched beside Ava with Missy clutching tightly to his leg. At least he knew she was there while he examined Ava. His mother, on the other hand, could be anywhere. He had to get help and get back to her. "Ava?"

She lifted her head and scooted up to sit, then gripped her head in both hands.

"Just hold on a sec. The dizziness should pass. You probably just moved too quickly." He kept a hand on Ava's shoulder, paid careful attention to Missy's weight against him, and scanned the area. An abandoned gas station was the only business in sight on the deserted stretch of highway. What were they even doing out there?

"Hey," a man yelled.

Jack whirled toward the voice as he tucked Missy next to her mother and slid in front of them.

Two men ran toward them from the direction of the hospital. One had a makeshift bandage pressed against his head.

The man in the lead, a burly guy in jeans and a black T-shirt, pointed toward him. "What's going on over there? Step away from the woman. Now."

Jack stood and put his hands out to the sides where they could clearly be seen but made no attempt to move from between the newcomers and Ava. "A woman and a child were attacked. I chased off the attacker, but I couldn't go after him and leave them alone."

The guy reached them and stopped, his breath coming in harsh gasps from running. He wiped the sweat beading his forehead with his wrist and peered around Jack to study Missy and Ava. "Are they all right?"

"I think so, but someone needs to call 911."

"Someone already did. We were just arriving to bring my buddy Ron here to the emergency room—" he gestured toward his friend with the bloody bandage against his head "—when an elderly woman came running across the parking lot yelling that a child was screaming and her boy went to help."

"Did you see where my mother went?" He had to get to her, but he couldn't leave Ava and Missy with strangers, even though the two newcomers, one obviously injured, were probably telling the truth.

"Don't worry about her. Ron's girlfriend had just met up with us, and she stayed back with your mom and called the police." The man crouched in front of Missy. "Are you okay, hon? Is this man telling the truth?"

She nodded. "Fireman Jack save me from the bad man."

"All right, sweetie. Don't you worry. The police are on their way, and we'll stay with you until they get here." He patted her head and stood to face Jack. "Sorry, man, but I had to be sure."

"No problem." Jack extended a hand, which the other man shook. "I'd have done the same thing."

A police cruiser pulled to the side of the road, with an ambulance not far behind.

Missy sat curled in Ava's lap as Ava told the officers what happened and the paramedics examined them.

Ron's girlfriend pulled up behind the police car, and she and Jack's mom got out and hurried to them.

Relief poured through him. "Are you all right, Mom?"

She nodded and slid into his arms.

Jack rested his chin on her head and watched Ava as the police questioned her. As he had the night before, he once again got the impression there was something she was hiding. She'd clearly been terrified last night, and his gut had told him it was more than someone breaking into the house.

He was pretty sure whatever happened the night before held the answers he sought. Burglars didn't typically stick around to take random sniper shots, and why risk hanging around a crime scene with cops swarming all over the place just to shoot a firefighter to prove a point? Unless he'd meant to kill him.

A shiver tore through Jack as he remembered the bullet whizzing past him, so close to Big Earl's head. Had Jack not been there, he had no doubt Earl would have been hit. No, this attacker wasn't playing games, wasn't trying to make a point. He'd had every intention of following through on the threat he'd made to Ava. And Ava knew it. But how? How could she be so sure he'd follow through if she didn't know who he was?

He'd suspected Ava was keeping secrets. And now that she'd been attacked twice in less than twenty-four hours, he was more certain than ever. But this time, he wasn't letting her go without answers.

FOUR

Ava strapped Missy into the car seat, then headed toward the beach with Jack practically glued to her bumper. Not that she really wanted to go to the church picnic with all that was going on, but where else could she go? Her house was obviously not safe, since her attacker knew where she lived. Nor was the shop, because he'd followed her that morning and knew where she worked. Apparently, even the hospital was no safe haven.

The thought of fleeing flickered briefly, but no way would she be able to shake Jack. Besides, she had no way to know if her stalker had planted a tracking device on the car. He'd found her the last time she'd tried to run; why would she think she could get away this time? No, better to go to the beach, hang out with Jack, Big Earl and Serena for a few hours, then find a way to slip away into the dark unnoticed. Without the car. Though the look in Jack's eye when he suggested the barbecue told her in no uncertain terms, he had questions. And he expected answers.

She comforted herself with the knowledge that between Missy and Jack's mother, they'd have their hands full, and there would be no time for him to interrogate her. If she were honest with herself, she had to admit to a certain amount of disappointment at that fact. It would have been nice to have someone to talk to, someone who would understand her fear, maybe even understand her reasons for running instead of going to the police for help and maybe confronting her husband's killer head-on.

She pulled into a parking space, and Jack parked next to her, not giving her an inch of breathing space. She scanned the lot, the street, the beach, everywhere she could see in search of her attacker, but she didn't spot the SUV. There was a train station not that far away. If she could slip away from the crowd at some point, she could make a run for it. All she'd have to do was make it onto the train into New York City, and from there she could lose herself anywhere in the world.

"Up, Mama," Missy whined and pulled at the car seat's harness. "Now."

"I'm coming, honey." Maybe this was a bad idea. Jack saw too much. What if he figured out what she intended to do? She laid her hand on the shifter, ready to shove it into Reverse and make a run for it.

A knock on her window startled her, and she jumped before hitting the button to disengage the locks.

Jack, ever the gentleman, opened the door for her. "Ready?"

As I'll ever be.

With one last look around, and a prayer they'd be safe amid a group of people, not only her friends and the other church members, but other beachgoers soaking up the last hour or two of sunshine, Ava got out of the car and went around to free Missy. The bonfire would be the perfect time to disappear. It would provide both the crowd and the cover of darkness she'd need to lose herself. Since trains ran every hour or so into the city, she could afford to wait, then, once she reached Penn Station, she'd grab the first train out in any direction. Better to leave that in God's hands anyway, since she had no clue where to go.

Jack held his mother's elbow and guided her toward Missy's side of the car.

Keeping Missy caged between the door and her leg, Ava leaned across the seat for the diaper bag. She usually loved heading down to the small park beside the beach for an hour or two whenever she could. Just one perk of living on an island. She'd miss it. Hefting the bag over her shoulder, she sighed. At least she could try to relax and enjoy the next couple of hours until darkness would aid her escape. Hopefully, Missy would be exhausted enough to fall asleep and grant Ava a reprieve from answering any questions until they'd moved on. "Ready?"

"Uh-huh." Missy turned toward the picnic area where Serena's teenage daughter, Kiara, was helping unload a cooler. "Hey, look. Kiara."

When Missy started to run ahead, Ava grabbed her hand and glanced at Jack.

He smiled and patted his mother's hand hooked through his elbow. "Go ahead. I'll catch up."

Careful to keep Missy even closer than usual, she scanned the entire area as they crossed the beach that bordered the Great South Bay. The section of high beach grass covering the small dunes blocked her view of the narrow strip of sand. Instead, she looked out over the bay toward the barrier island, searching for any spot a sniper might perch. The soft breeze whipped her hair across her face, and she took a moment to pull it back and tie it in the rubber band she always kept around her wrist.

"Hey." Serena waved from where she sat on one of the benches facing the playground. "Sit, relax, let Kiara run after Missy for a bit."

Since the playground was only a few feet away from them, Ava sat down on the edge of the bench beside Serena, poised to run if Missy needed her or if anything else happened. "Hi, Serena. I'm glad you guys came."

"Are you kidding me? The annual church picnic is akin to a night out on the town for me." She grinned. "The men will cook, and I have no dinner dishes. Everything goes in the garbage. It's a beautiful thing."

Ava laughed. She scanned the picnic area. "Earl's not here yet?"

"Not yet." Serena studied her for a moment, her gaze intense. "Are you okay?"

Since Ava had no idea what she'd heard, she kept things vague. If she didn't yet know about their encounter at the hospital, it would be better not to ruin their last evening together with the details. Besides, she needed a few minutes of peace to let her mind settle, see if she could come up with a better idea. "Yeah. I am."

"So… I saw Jack pull in behind you. Anything I should know?" She grinned and waggled her eyebrows, then gestured toward Jack.

He guided his mother slowly toward them, scanning the beach much as Ava had. How could she have even thought of asking him for help, when he obviously had his hands full, when any association with her could prove dangerous, not only for him, but for his mother too?

"What…oh…uh…" Ava shrugged. "No, I just… We ran into each other at the hospital and both happened to be coming this way. That's all—"

Serena's laughter cut her off. "Oh? Well, if you say so, but it's hard to miss the way he's looking at you."

Yeah, like she was a frightened animal who was about to bolt. "You can never have too many friends."

"Well, now, that's true enough, but there's nothing like having a best friend, that special someone to support you through all of life's tough times and share all of life's joys."

She'd had that with Liam. At least, she'd thought she did, before she'd found out he was keeping secrets—secrets that had gotten him killed and sent her on the run alone. Ugh. Blaming him wasn't fair. While it was true Liam hadn't confided in her about everything, he had told her he was looking into the arson and had left her the flight bag with everything she needed to flee. He'd even tried to do the right thing by going to the police. It wasn't his fault, and yet, sometimes she couldn't help being angry he was gone.

She'd never really talked to anyone about what it was like after Liam passed away—the pain, the anger, the loss of faith… When she'd come to Seaport, she and Serena had become fast friends, but the other woman had never pried after she'd told her Liam was a firefighter who'd been killed in the line of duty, and for that Ava was grateful.

Serena lifted her sunglasses to look at Ava then frowned. "Why don't you sit back? Relax? Kiara has her."

"I know." But she remained perched on the edge of

the bench, ready to move at a moment's notice, and watched Little Earl and Missy climb the ladder to the jungle gym.

Kiara followed them up.

The sinking sun still cast enough heat to warm her face. "When are Big Earl and the boys coming?"

"Earl had a few things to do at the firehouse, Alex and Regina were going to meet us here, and Carl should be getting off work anytime now." She glanced at her cell phone. "They should be here soon."

A black SUV rounded the corner and pulled into the small lot beside her car.

Ava lurched to her feet. Her heart thudded wildly.

Jack whirled toward the SUV, waited a moment, then waved and turned back to Ava and gave her a discreet head shake.

It wasn't the same car. She pressed a hand against her chest and tried to regain control of her breathing.

"Ava?" Serena stared in the direction Ava was looking, then stood and laid a hand on her arm. "Are you all right?"

"I am. I'm sorry, just jumpy I guess." She offered a shaky smile, the best she could do under the circumstances.

"Well, who can blame you after what happened."

Assuming she was referring to the break-in, Ava simply nodded.

"Hey, Serena." Jack kissed Serena's cheek. "My mom wants to rest and watch the kids play. Would you mind sitting with her a few moments while Ava and I take a walk on the beach?"

Serena shot Ava a knowing grin and turned to Jack's mother. "Of course I wouldn't mind. Come on, Miss

Jenny. Sit with me a bit, and let's let these two get to know each other better."

Ava started to protest, but the look in Jack's eyes had her holding her tongue. He'd saved her and Missy; she at least owed him an explanation, as much of one as she could give, anyway. Plus, this would be her last chance to thank him. But she would not wander so far that she couldn't keep an eye on Missy. Serena and Kiara were wonderful, and under ordinary circumstances she'd trust them with Missy completely, but these were far from ordinary circumstances. "Thank you, Serena."

The instant Jack turned to scan the horizon, Serena lifted a brow then winked at Ava.

Ah, man, just what she needed for her last few hours in Seaport: Serena in full matchmaker mode. She watched Missy going down the slide with her hands in the air. She seemed content for the moment, but it only took Missy a fraction of a second to find trouble.

"Go ahead." Serena shooed her. "I'll keep an eye on Mischief until you get back. I promise."

With one last glance at Missy, Ava turned and fell into step beside Jack.

He led her to the small wooden boardwalk that weaved a path through the beach grass and opened onto the small beach. The sun was a giant ball of orange, casting a beautiful glow across the surface of the gently lapping water. Shades of pink and lavender had begun to streak the sky. Since he stood in the sand at the boardwalk's edge without venturing any farther down the beach, she had to figure he understood her need to keep watch over Missy.

He stuffed his hands into the pockets of his jeans, thumbs hooked over the front. "I've always loved this time of day on the beach. Looks as if the water's on fire, doesn't it?"

Ava stiffened. She remembered standing on a beach very similar to this one, Liam at her side as he made the same observation. Now, the memories were nothing but a haze of pain and fear. "Yes, it does."

He glanced over his shoulder toward the playground then strolled a few feet farther down the beach, where small waves gently lapped against the shore. "You told Serena you were all right. Is that true?"

She bristled instinctively at the accusation that she'd lied, but what right did she have to be insulted when he was so accurate? Ava bent and picked up a whole moon snail shell, running her finger over the smooth, round, light purple and brown streaks on its surface.

"Ava, are you really all right?"

"Yes." She sighed. She'd had enough lies in her life. Even if Jack turned out to be nothing more than a passing acquaintance, he seemed genuinely concerned for her and Missy's safety. And he had saved their lives. "And no."

He turned to face her, started to reach toward her, then stopped and tucked his hand back into his pocket. "You seem to be shouldering quite a burden on your own. Isn't there anyone you can trust enough to talk to about what's going on?"

Trust. Wasn't that the key? She'd trusted Liam, and now he was gone. Liam had trusted someone, a friend most likely, and then the police, and that trust had cost him his life. She'd trusted God, eventually, after Liam was gone—trusted Him to lead her and Missy down a path that would keep them safe—and He had. Until now. Instinct once again had her prickling. Jack was way too observant, but also right. "I don't know what you're talking about."

He lifted one eyebrow and waited.

She turned to watch Missy, who'd moved from the slide to the monkey bars. Ava's gut knotted.

"Kiara is right underneath her." Jack captured her gaze and held it. "Please, Ava. I know there's something you're not telling me…or the police. Someone didn't break into your house for the sole purpose of telling you he was going to kill a firefighter then try to kidnap Missy at the hospital. Are you in some kind of trouble?"

The kindness in his eyes was her undoing, and her breath hitched.

Giving her a moment to collect herself, Jack pointed to a smooth piece of blue beach glass sticking out from among the seashells, seaweed and rocks scattered in a line in front of the boardwalk where the tide had deposited them on its way out.

Ava nodded and bent to pick it up, her lips closed tight over her clenched teeth. Her past wasn't something she talked about, and yet, somehow, she found she wanted to confide in Jack, to share the burden for just a few minutes, wanted his opinion and his advice. But was that selfish? Or did she owe him the truth? She was unable to look him in the eye. "I'm in trouble, and I have no idea how to get out of it. I don't know how much you've heard about my past…"

Not that there was much for him to have heard, but still, Seaport was a small town with a big gossip mill. The fact that her husband had been killed wasn't a secret, even if the circumstances were.

Jack laid a finger beneath her chin and lifted her gaze back to his. "I know you were hurt, but I don't know the circumstances. Other than a short conversation with Earl, I haven't tried to find out. I figured you'd tell me what you wanted to share when you were ready."

Ugh. Why did he have to be so understanding? She couldn't control the shakiness in her voice, but she did manage to keep the tears at bay. "My husband, Liam, was a firefighter."

Jack squeezed his eyes closed, obviously guessing this story had a tragic ending.

"The best day of my life was the day I found out I was pregnant with Missy." A chill raced through her. She'd never said these words aloud before, had never shared that day with anyone else. "It was also the worst. I was waiting for Liam to come home that night, so excited I could barely stand it. I'd made his favorite dinner, set the table with the good dishes, lit candles. Six hours. I'd waited six hours since I found out I was pregnant. The longest six hours of my life. I hadn't told anyone, because I wanted Liam to be the first to hear."

Her parents were already gone. Two more people she'd loved who'd been taken from her. And her brother, Tommy. She shied away from the thought. If she allowed thoughts of him in now, she'd lose her battle for control. "If I didn't tell Liam soon, I thought I'd surely burst. He would be so excited. We'd wanted a big family, had been trying to conceive a child for over a year. I watched the clock creep forward, knew he would be home any minute, and our lives would be forever changed. I checked the table again, just to be sure everything was perfect. It wasn't, of course, but I didn't know that then. Not yet, anyway."

She took a deep, shaky breath in. She'd need it to get through the rest, if she even could. For that little while, after the doctor had called, she'd allowed herself the reprieve from reality, from the fear of the bag Liam had packed, from the thought of him being in danger. A costly mistake. "A knock on the door startled me, but I hadn't been worried, figured maybe Liam had forgotten his key."

Tears rolled down her cheeks, but she ignored them, looked out over the water to avoid the sympathy she'd surely see in Jack's eyes, sympathy that might be her undoing. "Red and blue lights flashed across the walls through the open curtains. Still I hadn't been worried. Sirens and flashing lights were a common enough occurrence in our neighborhood. I prayed fleetingly that all of our neighbors were safe and sound, but nothing could deter from my happiness in that instant."

Until she reached the door. "I hesitated before I opened the door, asked who it was. When Captain Price called out, a small niggle of fear started to claw its way toward the surface of my mind. Though I knew the man from social events we'd attended over the years, Liam's captain never just stopped by the house. I thought… hoped…prayed maybe his visit had something to do with something Liam had been concerned about and peeked through the peephole to be sure it really was him. Several firefighters stood on the front porch with him, their expressions grim. One wiped his eyes with the back of his hand and clenched his teeth tight, his jaw straining under the pressure.

"And I knew. In that one fraction of a second, the expression on his fellow firefighter's face told me everything I needed to know. My life was completely and irrevocably changed. Forever. Part of me died in that instant."

She looked at Jack and found him watching her.

He remained silent, waiting, allowing her the room she needed to relive that tragic night.

"I was so angry. Angry with Liam for dying. Angry with God for taking him. Angry with myself for not calling him earlier in the day to tell him I was pregnant." She looked over at Missy, watched her laughing as Little Earl ran off toward Serena, needing to touch her, wanting to hug her close. "Not that it would have changed the outcome, but at least he'd have known he was going to be a father."

"I'm so sorry, Ava." Jack clenched his hands, but he kept them in his pockets.

"It wasn't until later that day that I found out what happened. Captain Price only told me he'd been killed." She'd been too mired in grief to care about the details at first, too lost in a sea of pain. Knowing he'd died in the line of duty while fighting a fire and saving lives was one thing, but finding out he'd been shot, probably because he'd been trying to stop an arsonist, was something else entirely. As soon as she'd found out he'd been murdered, it all fell into place. She should have seen it sooner, and probably would have if she'd been thinking clearly. But as it was, Liam had said he was going to the police, and then he was dead.

It took all the willpower Jack possessed and then some to keep his hands in his pockets instead of reaching out to her, but he was afraid he'd spook her if he did. She stared at the piece of beach glass caught between her fingers for a moment, giving him a brief chance to study her.

The dark circles around her eyes, the way her eyes

kept flicking from Mischief to the parking lot, to the surrounding picnic areas that had begun to swell with guests, the way she held herself so rigid, coiled to run at the slightest provocation, all spoke of a woman who was terrified. "Look, Ava, I can't promise I have the answers you're seeking, but why don't you give me a try? I know there's more to this story, suspect there's more to the circumstances surrounding Liam's death that you're not saying. And I think whatever it is has something to do with what has you so afraid now. I'm a good listener, and if nothing else, sometimes talking about your troubles out loud helps you find a solution you overlooked."

She lifted her gaze to his. "Do you believe in God, Jack?"

"Wha…uh…" The question caught him off guard. Though he didn't know exactly what he'd expected her to say, that hadn't been it.

"I'm sorry, I didn't mean to pry, I just—"

"No, no, it's okay, I don't mind answering. The question just took me by surprise." He searched for the right words to express his feelings. He was in his own sort of dilemma right now, worrying about his mother, even if his sister would be there by tonight since she'd left immediately after Darcy's call that their mom had been hurt. Although he'd tried to assure her things were okay, she'd insisted on coming. Not that he couldn't understand; he'd felt the same way when he'd gotten the call that she'd fallen, a call that had him taking a leave of absence, packing up what he needed and returning to Seaport immediately to care for her until further arrangements could be made.

As much as Jack wanted to return to the city, to

the life he'd created there, it seemed something kept pulling him toward Seaport. Was that God's will? Did God's plan for him follow a different path than he'd expected? "I do believe in God. And my faith has gotten me through some very tough times."

"Do you believe God sometimes puts people in our lives or…" She hesitated, but he checked Mischief while he waited for her to finish. No matter what she had or hadn't told the police, he had a suspicion the two of them were in some kind of danger. "I don't know… maybe alters the path we'd hoped to follow, expected to follow?"

The laugh blurted out before he could stop it.

Her cheeks reddened, and she returned to examining the shell and beach glass she still held.

"No, please, I'm sorry. It's just…well… I was having the exact same thought when you said it. My plan was to come out here for six months to take care of my mother until my sister's house sold and she could move back to Seaport full-time. Then I planned to return to New York City and pick up my life where I left off. But somehow, now, that plan doesn't appeal quite as much as it once did."

She glanced up then, and her cheeks flamed even redder.

He couldn't resist any longer. Reaching out, he slid the curls that had gone frizzy and fallen into her face behind her ear, let his fingers linger for just a moment in the softness of her hair, then lowered his hand. "Please, Ava, talk to me. I want to help. Who knows? Maybe God sent us to each other for some reason we don't yet understand. I want to help you if I can."

She nodded, dropped the shell and glass onto the

beach, brushed the sand from her hands, then took a deep breath and let it out slowly. "He died fighting a fire, but not from the fire. He was shot and killed."

Jack didn't know what to say. He knew the pain he'd suffered, his mother had suffered, when his father had been killed fighting a fire, but to have her husband murdered? Well, that was different. "Was his killer caught?"

She shook her head and checked Mischief again. "Would you mind walking back up toward the playground? It's starting to get crowded, and I can't always see Missy."

The panic in her eyes prodded him back up the boardwalk. "Sure, no problem. But will you tell me what's going on while we walk?"

"Before Liam was killed, he was investigating a string of fires he suspected were arson. He said he had proof of that, though he never told me what it was. He was going to tell me everything later that same evening, after he spoke with the police, but he never came home. Instead, there was the knock at the door and I was informed of his death." She paused and struggled to control her tears, to somehow keep them from spilling over.

His heart ached for her, for the pain she'd suffered, to be left grieving and alone under such tragic circumstances. "I'm so sorry, Ava. I can't imagine what that must have been like for you."

She nodded and sniffed. "Thank you."

Hoping she wouldn't take the gesture the wrong way but wanting to lend her strength, he took her hand in his as they crossed the grassy field to the playground. He'd only have another moment before they were back with everyone else. "What did the police say?"

"Nothing, because I never called them."

"Why not?"

"Liam didn't feel comfortable going to the police. He didn't trust them for some reason, though he never got to explain why. Then, when he finally told me he was going to them with whatever he had, he was killed. When I first found out he was gone, I was in shock, scared, grieving… I needed time to think about what to do. I searched the house, searched the flight bag he had packed and had ready for us."

The fact he'd packed a flight bag spoke volumes about the state Liam had been in, but with only seconds left for her to finish her story, he didn't dare interrupt to ask about it.

"But I couldn't find the evidence he was talking about. And then, that night, while I was still trying to come to terms with his loss, there was another fire. And our home burned to the ground behind me while I ran for my life with nothing but that bag and a sniper shooting at me."

His grip on her hand tightened.

"I fled Florida and made my way north, never staying anywhere more than a few months, just in case the shooter came after me. And I never looked back. I was too scared to contact the police. I couldn't find anything about Liam's death in the local papers I looked up online, except that he was killed fighting a fire. I figured the fact there was no mention he was murdered spoke volumes, so I just kept on running until I finally ended up here. For the first time, I thought I might finally have decided on a home for Missy and me. And then he found us, all because of a picture in the paper. He broke into the house, told me he'd…" She sobbed softly. "He insisted I had a flash drive he wanted, which I assume is the evidence Liam had on him. If I hadn't volunteered at the hospital, hadn't tried to be a part of the community here, maybe Missy and I would still be safe."

And he knew in that instant, by the look in her eye, exactly what Ava planned to do. And he had no intention of letting her do it.

FIVE

Ava lifted Missy onto the swing, then pulled the swing back a little and let Missy fly. "Hold on tight."

Missy giggled wildly. "Weee…"

When she came back, Ava pushed again.

Missy's hair flew out behind her as she leaned her head back.

Fear clutched Ava's throat at the thought of Missy falling. "Hold on, Missy."

Her laughter floated back to Ava on the evening breeze blowing across the bay. "I know."

She had to relax. Her conversation with Jack, while liberating in a way, had also reminded her of the stark terror she'd felt while on the run, before she'd found what she'd thought could be a home, and now her nerves were strung taut. Missy's laughter helped soothe them, but the reminder she couldn't stay here, couldn't build a life for them, brought an ache to her heart she didn't think would ever go away. She'd worked so hard to achieve her dream of finding a true home for her and Missy, only to have it ripped away by a man capable of such senseless violence.

"Higher!" Missy pumped her pudgy legs with every push.

He could only take her life away if she allowed it. No

matter what the circumstances, she still had a choice. She could stay and fight.

"Help me, God, please," she whispered. *I'm so lost. I trust You, trust You to lead me in the right direction, but I don't know what that direction is. Did You allow this man to come back into our lives to push me down another path? Or did You send Jack to help me stand and fight this time, to do the right thing so no one else will get killed?*

But no answers came, no sense of enlightenment, no urge to stay or run. That being the case, it was time to say her goodbyes and disappear.

"Slide." Missy squirmed and turned on the seat, then reached out a hand to Ava.

"Don't let go." The swing twisted, and Ava's heart lurched. She grabbed the swing, stopping the motion instantly as Missy jumped off and into her arms. Ava hugged her close—a moment longer than necessary— then set her on her feet and followed her to the slide that sat on the edge of the playground closest to the woods.

"She gets bored fast, huh?"

She turned to find Jack standing right next to her. A sign? It seemed every time she was poised to run something blocked her path. No, not something. Jack. "And she swings longer than anything else."

His smile shot straight to her heart.

What was she going to do? It had felt good to talk to him, to have someone to share her burden with, to have a friend she could trust without fear of putting him in danger, since he'd already put himself there to save her and Missy. Except, if she were honest with herself, she'd have to admit to that small spark of attraction she felt every time he was near. Maybe she could ignore it and simply enjoy his company.

They stood together, side by side, and watched Missy climb the ladder. For just a moment, Ava allowed the thought of a normal life to flicker through her mind, a life where she could hang around Seaport and get to know Jack better.

"Ava, please, let me help you."

She stiffened and took a step away from him.

"I know a cop, a good cop. His name is Gabe, and he was at your house last night. Let me talk to him, off the record, and see what options you have." He stepped in front of her, laid a finger beneath her chin and lifted her gaze to his. "Please, Ava. Don't run. At least, not yet."

Tears burned, threated to spill over. She fought them off. The last thing she needed was to draw attention to herself. Instead, she looked away.

"Look, Ava, I'm going to be perfectly honest with you. I have no idea where my life is headed right now, and I know you're pretty much in the same position, and normally, I wouldn't say anything like this, but…" He took a deep breath and let it out slowly, then raked a hand through his thick hair. "I can't explain what it is exactly, but I feel a connection with you, have since the first moment I met you. Don't get me wrong. It's not a romantic connection, but it's something, like I'm meant to help you, if you can understand what I mean. I don't want you to leave, and I have a strong suspicion that's what's about to happen. Wherever the future may lead, I know with absolute certainty that at this moment, I want to stay with you, want to keep you and Missy safe, want to help you get the justice Liam deserves, and I want to keep this man from harming anyone else. Please, will you at least give me a chance to try to help you?"

She kept her eyes averted, had to if she was going to have any hope of resisting his offer. A shadow shifted behind a row of bushes bordering the side street she'd planned to use to make her escape. She narrowed her gaze, trying to bring the dark object into focus, but it was no use. The setting sun had already begun to cast shadows too deep for her gaze to penetrate.

"I'm sorry if I said something wrong." He spoke quietly.

Her heart ached, and she shifted to watch Missy, once again at the top of the slide. She shook her head. How could she explain to him that she didn't want to involve anyone else in this? Couldn't bear the thought of anyone else she cared for being taken from her? There was no way to explain she'd buried a large part of herself with Liam, and even before that, with her parents, with Tommy. "You didn't say anything wrong."

She studied him for a moment as he watched Missy play, a wistful expression she doubted he was aware of on his face, and she had to turn away.

When he next spoke, his voice was closer, right by her side. "I won't pry. If there are things you're not comfortable talking about, just say so. I'll always respect that."

Oh, man… Why did he have to be so understanding? He was making it so hard to just walk away.

"Mama, look." Missy waved from the top of the platform, holding on to a bar above the rock wall.

Why did they make these stupid playgrounds so high?

"I can do like the big kids."

She leaned out through the gap, and Ava read the intent in her eyes an instant before she let go and jumped off. "Nooo... Missy."

The sound of an engine revving reached her an instant before a dark SUV plowed through the row of bushes and bounced over the grass bordering the playground, headed straight for them.

Time slowed down. She screamed as she ran for Missy, but there was no way she'd make it.

Jack dove in front of her, grabbing Missy by the arm a split second before she hit the sand. As the truck slammed into the rock wall she'd been standing on, Jack rolled out of the way with her.

Ava dove to the side to avoid being hit seconds before the truck got caught up in the slide and finally came to a stop.

A man she didn't know ran toward the SUV, then ripped the door open. He reached in and grabbed something that made the engine stop racing before he shifted the truck into Park and turned it off. He scratched his head and looked around. "There's no one in it. Just a stick wedged onto the gas pedal."

"Are you all right?" Ava fell to her knees and felt Missy's arms and legs, certain something had to be broken.

Missy sobbed, burying her head against Ava's chest. "I sor-ry."

The muffled apology broke her heart.

Jack stood over her, Big Earl and Serena on either side of him.

"Is she all right?"

"Is she hurt?"

"I think she just got scared." Ava sucked in a shaky

breath, then set Missy back a little and wiped her eyes. "Are you hurt, honey?"

She shook her head, her curls bouncing into her face.

Ava brushed them back. "I'm sorry I yelled. I just got scared."

A tentative smile formed through Missy's tears.

"We've talked about this before. Are you supposed to do what the big kids do?"

Missy glanced up from beneath her lashes and shook her head.

Torn between the desire to make sure Missy understood she shouldn't do dangerous things and the fact that if she hadn't jumped when she did, the SUV would certainly have injured her, Ava forced a smile. "Come here."

Launching herself into Ava's arms, Missy wrapped her arms around her neck.

"I'm just glad you weren't hurt. You are okay, right?"

"Yup." Stepping back, Missy wiped the rest of the tears from her face. "Can I play more now?"

Ava couldn't help the sigh that escaped. With no thought whatsoever to the SUV that had crashed through the playground, Missy was ready to move on to whatever adventure awaited her next. This child was without doubt the biggest blessing she'd ever received, and the biggest trial.

Missy clasped her hands together against her chest. "Please."

"Let's just sit on the bench for a minute and make sure you're okay." And wait for the police to get there so she could try to answer their questions. Because she was going to this time. Enough playing around. Thankfully, Jack had saved Missy, but what if there had been

other children on the playground? That made her pause
and pull Missy tighter while she searched her surroundings for anyone suspicious. What if he knew Missy was
the only child playing at that moment? There had been
others before the SUV had come through, but just then,
it had only been Missy.

Missy glanced longingly at the wrecked playground,
then shrugged.

Jack held out a hand, and Ava only hesitated a moment before taking it and letting him help her to her feet.

Big Earl clapped Jack on the back, then laughed and
shook his head, easing some of the tension. "Nice re-
flexes."

"That one's a handful and a half." Even though she
laughed, Serena squeezed Ava's arm in a silent gesture of support.

"No kidding." Ava turned to Jack as the wail of sirens grew louder. "I don't know how I can ever thank
you."

"I'm just glad she's okay." He was silent for a minute
as they crossed the small patch of grass, not seeming to
know what to say. "Does she do stuff like that a lot?"

Ava let out a short laugh. She couldn't help it. "Yup.
On a regular basis."

"I realize that's not usually a good thing, but in this
instance, it worked out for the best." Jack stuffed his
hands in his pockets and looked around.

While Ava appreciated the fact that he didn't push her
about going to the police, she could read his thoughts in
his hesitation, and she knew what she had to do…before
anyone else got hurt…and before she fled Seaport for
good. She wouldn't be able to stay, not after speaking
to the police and telling them whatever she knew, be-

cause the killer said he would come after Missy if she did. Liam had been killed right after talking to the police, and her attacker had threatened her, but how could she risk more lives without trying to help?

Right or wrong, she'd walked away without putting up a fight to avenge Liam's death, but he'd already been gone. Coming forward wasn't going to save him. But she couldn't stand by and let anyone else be killed because she was afraid to speak up. She wouldn't. "I'm going to tell the police what's going on. Hopefully, it'll be your friend Gabe that shows up, but even if it's not, I can't keep this inside anymore, can't risk an innocent bystander getting hurt because I kept my mouth shut."

His posture relaxed as he reached for her, pulled her and Missy close for a hug, his hand smoothing Ava's hair as he whispered, "You're doing the right thing."

She just nodded against him, absorbing his strength, allowing herself this single moment to accept the comfort being offered, to indulge in the one moment of safety his strong embrace offered.

The loud peal of the fire alarm calling the volunteers to the nearby firehouse ended her moment of peace.

Big Earl, along with several other volunteers, ran for the parking lot.

Jack hesitated, vibrating with energy as his gaze landed on his mother.

"Go. I'll let your mom know what's going on and see if she can stay with Serena for a bit." Ava shooed him toward his truck. It was time for her to go anyway, after she kept her promise to get Miss Jenny to Serena then spoke to the police, and the best way to do that would be to let Jack go.

"Thank you. I'll call Darcy on my way to the firehouse to stay with her."

Whatever else he said got swallowed up by the wind as he ran for the parking lot. With an all-volunteer fire department, every second's delay could be dangerous. When the fire whistle blew, any of the firemen who were available dropped everything and ran, blue lights flashing on their dashboards as they flew toward the firehouse. Whoever was manning the firehouse would have the trucks running and the big garage doors open.

Jack climbed into his SUV and backed out of his parking spot. As he started forward, Ava noticed a man standing across the street, arms folded over his chest, one ankle crossed over the other, shoulder resting comfortably against the streetlight pole. Though he wore a sweatshirt with the hood pulled low enough to conceal most of his features in shadow, she could feel the weight of his stare, his gaze unflinching, even when she looked back. She shivered and wrapped her arms tighter around her daughter, hugging Missy against her, gaze riveted on the stranger as Jack's SUV disappeared around the corner and he rushed off into danger.

The man reached into his pocket and fished out a cell phone. Keeping his gaze pinned on Ava, he hit a button and held the phone to his ear.

An instant later, Ava's cell phone rang. She pulled it out of her pocket and read Unknown Number on the screen. Certain it was going to be him, she answered. She tried to say hello, but her mouth had gone completely dry and she couldn't force the word out.

The man watching her grinned as a police car pulled up and stopped. "I'd be very careful if I were you. Your pit bull's not here now, gone off to fight a fire, just like dear old Liam did all those years ago. Keep your mouth shut and get me what I asked for. Your time's almost up."

The man stuck the phone back into his pocket and nodded to the officer getting out of his cruiser as he strolled away.

The man couldn't possibly have set the fire Jack had just been called to, not if he was busy rigging his SUV to plow through the playground. And then it hit her: he wasn't working alone. How many people were involved in this? Her gaze ricocheted around her. His accomplice could be anyone, anywhere. Or perhaps more than one person was involved. But why? What did they have to gain? She started backing away.

"Ma'am?" She recognized the officer from the night before. Sam something, not Jack's friend. But it didn't matter anyway. What if someone in the police department was involved with this guy? Or someone in the crowd that had gathered to witness the drama reported back to him every word Ava said?

Since she didn't have the evidence he was searching for, she couldn't give him what he wanted anyway. Which left her no choice but to run. Or at least try, since escaping hadn't worked out for her so far.

"Ma'am?" Officer Sam Something frowned. "Are you all right?"

Ava forced a smile and prayed for forgiveness, because there was no way she was saying anything.

Jack and Earl jumped out of the first fire truck to arrive on the scene. Jack was already sizing up the situation as he shrugged into the remainder of his gear and grabbed his Halligan—a long bar with one forked end and a blade and a pick at the other end—from the truck. Small crowds had gathered haphazardly around the building, blocking some of the parking lot, standing on the lawn, some too close. Several police officers worked to move everyone back.

The chief—who'd arrived before any of the trucks in his SUV and would serve as the Incident Commander— jogged toward them from the rear of the building, having just completed his assessment.

Four attached, three-story units seemed to be in immediate danger. Smoke billowed from the windows of the end unit, which appeared to be fully engulfed in flames. Black smoke filled the air, pouring from the open front door of the second unit in line. The last two seemed to be okay for the moment.

Jack double-checked his self-contained breathing apparatus—SCBA.

A woman burst from the front door of the second unit, stumbled down the stairs and fell, hitting her chin on the sidewalk.

Jack ran toward her.

She struggled to regain her footing, tears streaming through the soot covering her face. Sobbing and straining to breathe, she tried to talk.

"You have to calm down, ma'am." Jack gripped her arm. "Are you hurt?"

She shook her head and pointed toward the unit she'd come from. "My baby…" She wheezed between sobs. "I've looked everywhere, and I can't find him."

Oh, no. "Could he have gotten out?"

She was already shaking her head before he could finish the sentence. "No. He knows not to go outside alone."

Jack turned and yelled over his shoulder. "We have a kid inside!" As he heard Earl relay the message, he turned back to the woman. "How old is he?"

She sucked in a shaky breath and coughed. "Six."

It hit him like a punch in the gut, as it often did unexpectedly. Six, the same age Matthew would now be. "What's his name?"

The woman grabbed his shoulder straps and shook him. "Please, you have to find him. He's scared of fire." She broke down and probably would have collapsed to the ground if he hadn't caught her as sobs racked her body and sent her into a coughing fit.

He took her upper arms firmly and set her back up. "His name. What's his name?"

"Connor."

A police officer reached them and took the woman from him.

It made no difference the others were preparing to enter the building as he took the time to gain valuable information. Urgency still beat at him, begged him to act. "Where in the house?"

She shook her head. "I don't know. I was in the kitchen when the fire started."

"You're sure he couldn't have gotten out, ma'am?" Before she even answered, the police officer spoke softly into his radio, no doubt ordering a search.

"No, no, no. Connor!" she screamed and started back toward the building.

The officer restrained her. "Come on, ma'am. Let the firefighters find him."

Earl reached his side. "Let's go."

Jack tucked the Halligan in his SCBA strap, pulled off his helmet, fit his mask into place and put the helmet back on. He pulled on his gloves then yanked the Halligan back out. His radio crackled to life with calls for ventilation as they jogged toward the building.

Thoughts of Matthew filled his head, begged for attention. Was his little boy safe? Happy? When Carrie had walked away, she'd cut all ties, hadn't kept in touch, hadn't even sent a recent picture or an update on how Matthew was, despite the promises she'd made when he'd agreed to walk away.

He wondered what Ava would think of Carrie's request. Would she ever ask someone who loved her, loved her child, to walk away? He had no doubt she would if she thought it was the best thing for Missy, but he also had a feeling if it had been Ava who'd asked him to walk away, she'd have kept her promise to send updates. He shook off the thoughts. He needed to keep his thoughts in the moment instead of ricocheting around in the past, or worse, gravitating toward Ava and that mischievous little girl of hers.

A second truck arrived, and Jack stepped over a hose as firefighters pulled more hoses from the trucks, hooked them to the hydrants and dragged them across the lawn. A ladder already stood to the side of a second-story window, another firefighter standing behind it ready to assist.

Black smoke poured from the top of the open front door, rolling along the underside of the porch roof before billowing out into the sky. The hoses came to life, water surging through the door, beating back the flames as a team entered the first floor.

Jack climbed the ladder, praying desperately the child had escaped and hidden outside. When he reached the top, he kept to the side of the window, shattered it with the Halligan and then used the tool to clear the remaining shards from the frame. He felt around the floor beneath him with the Halligan. Nothing in the way, and the floor seemed solid. He climbed over the ledge with Earl at his back and urgency begging him to move faster.

Darkness enveloped him. Crawling on his hands and knees, keeping below the smoke that was impeding his vision, he swept the floor in front of him with the Halligan. "Connor!"

He held his breath and listened for an answer. Nothing. The king-sized bed he checked under before standing told him they were probably in the master bedroom.

"Connor!" Earl yelled beside him, and he could hear the child's name being called from downstairs in the background of the radio. They moved through the room quickly, searching thoroughly, with no indication the child was inside.

For some reason thoughts of Ava came unbidden. Was she safe? He couldn't bear the thought of her in danger. The image of her fleeing flames, having just lost her husband, knowing she was carrying a child, ratcheted up his heart rate even further. Her courage touched him in a way few things had, but he tucked the thoughts away for another time. Or never.

When they reached the closed door, Jack cleared his mind of all but the moment and pressed a hand against it. He stood to the side and pushed it open. Smoke filled the short hallway. A closed door stood to his left. He pulled it open and reached in, stretching the Halligan to the back of a linen closet, then closed it again. Empty.

Earl moved past him and into the bathroom directly

across the hall. He returned after a quick but thorough search. "No victims."

Together they made their way down the hallway toward the back of the house, keeping careful track of the direction they were heading and noting any potential exits as they moved. Flames licked the stairway walls, and showers of sparks rained down in every direction.

Jack paused at a closed door at the end of the hall. Sweat trickled down his back.

As Earl pushed it open, Jack entered the little boy's bedroom and had to slam the door on the sudden barrage of memories even as he closed the door behind him. He dropped to his knees, following the same procedure they had in the first bedroom.

Toys littered the floor. When Jack turned to the left, he toppled a pile of blocks that had been stacked beside a closed toy box. He shoved the lid open and reached inside, grabbed the little boy beneath the arms and yanked him out, then cradled him against his chest. "I've got him."

Earl radioed for help, relayed their position as Jack checked the boy's breathing.

Glass shattered from across the room as a window was broken from the outside and cleared.

With a strong hold on Jack's jacket, Earl hauled him to his feet, and they started across the room.

A groan was all the warning Jack had as the floor buckled then caved. Jack dove back toward the wall, curling his body protectively over the boy.

Earl's weight pressed against him for a moment, then disappeared.

"Mayday!" Jack turned, frantic to find his partner. His friend. "Firefighter down!"

His worst nightmare erupted around him. With the child in his arms, and Earl missing, Jack had never felt more helpless. Praying for strength and guidance, he whirled back to where he'd last seen Earl. If he allowed indecision to paralyze him, they were all as good as dead. "Earl!"

He strained to listen to the sounds from the radio, to sort out if Earl's voice could be heard between the other voices. Nothing. On his knees, using one arm to cradle the child close, Jack felt along the floor with the Halligan. "Earl!"

At least the entire floor hadn't collapsed. He hoped fleetingly no one had been in the room beneath them.

"Give me the boy."

Oh, thank you! He thrust the child into another firefighter's arms. He in turn passed him to the next guy in line waiting on the ladder. With the boy safely out of harm's way, and help beside him, Jack returned to his search. Earl had been right next to him. Standing almost shoulder to shoulder. He had to still be there.

Jack felt along the floor, listening for the piercing alarm from Earl's PASS device, which should sound if he was still for more than a few moments. If he wasn't moving, the alarm should've sounded by now. Jack inched farther into the room, skirting the flames that were already being doused by hoses through the broken window. Earl's alarm sounded, closer than he'd expected. He rounded the far side of the hole, and his hand landed on Earl's arm.

"I've got him." A tidal wave of relief tore through Jack, shredding almost every ounce of his hard-won battle for control. He squinted, straining to see through the smoke. "All right, buddy. We're gonna get you out of here."

Grabbing hold of the straps of Earl's air tank, he started to pull him out. Within a second or two—though it felt more like a lifetime—help arrived at his side. They lifted Earl and carried him the remainder of the way across the room. Jack practically dove through the window onto the ladder, and someone hoisted Earl after him, feet down. With his knee between Earl's legs to keep him from sliding down, and his hands under his arms to steady him, Jack descended the rungs as quickly as possible, careful not to miss one and send Earl tumbling.

"Three, two..." Since he couldn't look down, the firefighter standing behind the ladder, holding it steady, counted out his last steps. "You're down!"

Jack dragged Earl farther from the building and lowered him to the ground. He sat behind him, straddling his head, and rolled Earl onto his back, then pulled Earl's head into his lap and positioned him so Earl's tank rested between Jack's legs. Jack ripped his helmet and mask off. "Earl!"

SIX

Ava stood outside the bounce house while Missy jumped around, ricocheting off the walls with some of the other kids. Laughter filled the air, and Ava forced a smile when Missy waved to her, but her stomach was in knots. Although the playground had been roped off and was off-limits, the kids enjoyed themselves playing on the inflatable bounce houses and slides. Obstacle courses had been rented and set up on the field beneath spotlights. But tension ran high among the adults gathered at the church picnic, even though none of them had a clue that a stranger was stalking Ava, watching them, prepared to kill with no hesitation and no regard for collateral damage.

Many of them, even those from neighboring towns, had family members who'd been called away to the fire at the condos, and rumor had it, the fire was a bad one. That rumor had Ava waiting around for word when she should be halfway to New York City already.

Her hand shook as she tucked her hair behind her ear. She liked Jack. A lot. But she didn't know if her nerves could take this. She tried to tell herself her fear for him was only guilt that she'd been the cause of him and all the others being put in danger. And that was partly true. But waiting around while he was in danger might be more than she could deal with either way. And no matter how many times she tried to convince herself he was just a kind man, she knew it wasn't true. Like so many others in Seaport, Jack had wormed his way past her guard and become a friend.

Keeping one eye on Missy and the other on a few women who were listening to the call over a scanner, Ava searched for a way out. But did she really want to run? Or did she want to stay in Seaport, build relationships? Was she ready for any kind of relationship, friendship or otherwise? Would she ever be able to open her heart again, knowing someone she loved could be taken from her at any moment? At one time, the answer would have been a definite no. Now, since meeting Jack, she wasn't so sure.

A dull throb started at her temples. As much as she wanted to be a part of this community, wanted to be friends with Serena and Big Earl and Jack, she couldn't be so selfish. Look at these people, all gathered together in fear for their loved ones, all because of her, because she was selfish enough to have wanted a family.

She massaged her pounding temples. This shouldn't be such a hard decision. Other people didn't have so much trouble deciding what path to follow.

Well…other people hadn't lost everyone they'd ever loved. Her gaze shot to Missy. Almost everyone. Fear gripped her throat at the thought of anything happening to Missy, but she fought off the urge to pull her out of the bounce house and into her arms. Barely.

Besides, hadn't her decision already been made when she hadn't shared what she knew with the police offi-

Get ready to relax and indulge with your FREE BOOKS and more!

**Claim up to FOUR NEW BOOKS & TWO MYSTERY GIFTS –
absolutely FREE!**

Dear Reader,

We both know life can be difficult at times. That's why it's important to treat yourself so you can relax and recharge once in a while.

And I'd like to help you do this by sending you this amazing offer of up to FOUR brand new full length FREE BOOKS that WE pay for.

This is everything I have ready to send to you right now:

Try **Love Inspired® Romance Larger-Print** books and fall in love with inspirational romances that take you on an uplifting journey of faith, forgiveness and hope.

Try **Love Inspired® Suspense Larger-Print** books where courage and optimism unite in stories of faith and love in the face of danger.

Or **TRY BOTH!**

All we ask in return is that you answer 4 simple questions on the attached Treat Yourself survey. You'll get **Two Free Books** and **Two Mystery Gifts** from each series you try, *altogether worth over $20*! Who could pass up a deal like that?

Sincerely,

Pam Powers

Harlequin Reader Service

Treat Yourself to Free Books and Free Gifts.

Answer 4 fun questions and get rewarded.

We love to connect with our readers! Please tell us a little about you...

▶ DETACH AND MAIL CARD TODAY! ▶

	YES	NO
1. I LOVE reading a good book.		
2. I indulge and "treat" myself often.		
3. I love getting FREE things.		
4. Reading is one of my favorite activities.		

TREAT YOURSELF • Pick your 2 Free Books...

Yes! Please send me my Free Books from each series I select and Free Mystery Gifts. I understand that I am under no obligation to buy anything, as explained on the back of this card.

Which do you prefer?

❏ **Love Inspired® Romance Larger-Print** 122/322 IDL GRDP
❏ **Love Inspired® Suspense Larger-Print** 107/307 IDL GRDP
❏ **Try Both** 122/322 & 107/307 IDL GRED

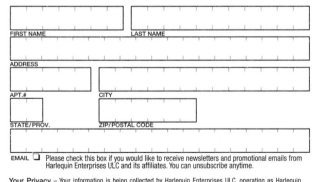

FIRST NAME   LAST NAME

ADDRESS

APT.#   CITY

STATE/PROV.   ZIP/POSTAL CODE

EMAIL ❏ Please check this box if you would like to receive newsletters and promotional emails from Harlequin Enterprises ULC and its affiliates. You can unsubscribe anytime.

© 2022 HARLEQUIN ENTERPRISES ULC ™ and ® are trademarks owned by Harlequin Enterprises ULC. Printed in the U.S.A.

LI/SLI-520-TY22

cers? Of course, she could still ask Jack to contact Gabe and tell him everything.

A flurry of activity caught her attention, pulling her from things she'd rather not contemplate anyway. More people gathered around the scanner. One woman held her bottom lip between her teeth, another twisted a band around and around her left ring finger. A man ran a hand over his near crew cut. The slight undercurrent of tension she'd felt earlier had blossomed. Something was wrong.

"Missy." Ava leaned into the bounce house and gestured for Missy to come to her.

"What?" Missy kept jumping, but at least she started toward Ava.

"Come here, babe." Urgency pummeled her, but she kept it at bay, not wanting to scare Missy. "I want to get something to drink."

"Can I have a juice box?"

"Sure, honey."

With one final bounce, Missy jumped into her arms.

Ava staggered under the weight, then set her down and held her hand as she crossed the lawn to the coolers beneath the table where the group continued to grow. Keeping Missy tucked between her leg and the cooler, she lifted the top for Missy to choose her drink. Ava scanned the small crowd. "Is something wrong?"

A woman she didn't recognize looked up with tears in her eyes. Her eyes darted toward Missy for an instant before she lowered her voice. "There was a partial collapse. Firefighters are trapped inside."

Jack! An iron fist clutched her heart and squeezed. She couldn't force air into her lungs. "Is everyone all right?"

She shook her head. "We don't know yet."

Serena walked toward her carrying a large tray filled with sandwiches. When her gaze met Ava's she slowed and her eyes went wide.

Ava understood the reaction, the same reaction she'd had when she looked through the peephole and found firefighters at her door the day Liam was killed, the almost unbearable urge to flee. Because if you didn't hear the words, it wouldn't be real.

Missy tugged at her shirt. "Mama!"

The aggravation in Missy's voice pulled Ava out of her stupor. Obviously, she'd called her more than once. "I'm sorry, honey. What did you say?"

"Help." She held up the juice box and the straw she'd ripped from its side.

"Sure." She shook her head to clear some of the fog. She unwrapped the straw and popped it through the top of the drink, then handed it back to Missy just as Serena reached her side.

"What happened?"

Ava's heart ached for Serena. Earl was her husband, the father of her children. They'd spent more of their lives together than they had apart. "A partial collapse. With firefighters trapped."

Serena squeezed her eyes closed and took a few deep breaths. When she finally opened them again, she seemed in control. "Okay, then."

She reached for Ava's hand, then extended her other hand to Miss Jenny, who was standing next to her. Others joined in, forming a circle as they lowered their heads in prayer.

Missy leaned her head against the front of Ava's leg, thumb in her mouth.

"Mom!" Serena's oldest son jogged toward them.

Ava gripped her hand tighter as everyone turned.

Two firefighters followed Alex across the field.

When Alex reached his mother, he put an arm around her shoulder and waited for the firefighters.

Serena stiffened but held her ground. She waited without saying a word or turning her gaze from the approaching firefighters.

Memories assailed Ava. She lowered her gaze, unable to take the hurt in the men's eyes as they crossed to Serena, no doubt to impart bad news. Her grip on Serena's hand tightened.

Then she realized Jack's mother stood on Serena's other side, staring at the approaching men as well. Maybe it wasn't Serena they were coming to talk to.

"Serena." The first firefighter to reach her, Ben Stevens, took her free hand in his. "Earl's been hurt."

"Hurt?"

"He was inside when the floor collapsed. He's on his way to the hospital."

She kept her composure. "How bad?"

"I don't know yet. He was unconscious when Jack brought him out."

Relief surged through Ava, slumping her shoulders, followed by a wave of guilt. Jack must be okay, but Earl wasn't. She lifted Missy into her arms. "Come on, Serena. I'll take you to the hospital."

Serena nodded and started forward, her movements stiff, as one of the other women wrapped an arm around Miss Jenny.

Somehow, Ava got Serena to the car and headed toward the hospital.

As the miles passed—slower than Ava would have

thought possible—Serena stayed quiet and stared out the window. Ava understood and left her to her thoughts. Unfortunately, when Missy dozed off in the car seat, Ava was alone with her thoughts as well.

This time her memories brought her back further than Liam's death, to another painful time. Liam had been killed instantly. At least she could rest with the knowledge he hadn't suffered.

Her brother, Tommy, had suffered greatly. She'd never forget the phone call that had woken her barely a year after she'd moved out of the home where she'd grown up. Her parents and Tommy had been in a bad accident on their way back from a weekend trip upstate. A trip Ava would have been on if she hadn't gotten a new job that prevented her from leaving town that weekend.

Ava wiped tears from her cheeks as she pulled up to the emergency room doors. "Go, Serena. I'll find a parking spot and meet you inside."

"Thank you." Serena squeezed her hand before jumping from the car and running through the automatic doors.

Ava circled the lot, passing a number of open parking spots that were filling rapidly. News of an injured firefighter would spread, and people would come, offer support, because that's what people in small communities did. They were a family. And Ava had no right to stick around and put them in danger. She started out of the lot. But she couldn't leave without knowing if Big Earl would be okay. She couldn't leave without standing by Serena's side in case she needed her. Ava had been forced to deal with Liam's death alone. She couldn't leave Serena. She wouldn't. Biting back a scream so as not to wake Missy, she pulled into a spot close to the exit.

She'd check on Serena, and then she was out of there. Serena might not understand why she'd left, but it was safest for everyone. She parked and jumped out of the car, hefting the flight bag over her shoulder in case she couldn't make it back, and carefully lifted Missy into her arms. The longer she stayed asleep, the easier it would be to make a run for it.

Jack sat slumped in a chair in the hospital waiting room, elbows resting on his knees, head down, hands clasped over the back of his head. The adrenaline rush had finally started to subside, leaving him shaky.

"Jack."

He looked up and found Patrick Ryan—one of the other firefighters who'd helped him pull Earl out—standing in front of him.

"The little boy's gonna be all right, man." He clapped Jack on the shoulder. "I figured you'd want to know."

Too choked with emotion to speak, Jack simply nodded his appreciation. Pat would understand, just like he'd understood Jack would need to know and had gone to find out the child's status. But he'd never understand the pain Jack had suffered when he'd looked down into that little boy's face to be sure he was breathing and had seen a child the size his own son would be now, a child who'd grown and gone on with no memory of the man who'd once loved him like his own.

Pat crossed the room and stood against the wall since there were no seats left in the crowded waiting room. As it turned out, it hadn't only been Earl caught in the collapse. Two other firefighters had been on the first floor when the ceiling caved in on them. One of them was in surgery now, and the other was still having tests run. Thankfully, they'd been able to pull them out quickly. Otherwise, the results would have been much worse.

Jack rubbed his hands over his face and sat up, needing to move to rid himself of the images that were tormenting him. He looked around the room at the group of men and women assembled there. Volunteer firefighters from their own house as well as from several surrounding towns. A good group of people, with a strong sense of community. A family of sorts. The realization that being part of a small, close-knit community wasn't such a bad thing brought confusion as much as anything else.

Maybe it was time to think about settling down and returning. The sentiment slammed into him with all the force of a punch in the gut. *Home.* No matter how long he'd lived in the city, his apartment there had never really been home. Every time he returned to Seaport to visit his mother, the feeling of coming home overwhelmed him. He'd grown up with Pat Ryan, had played Little League with him and his older brother, Brad, for years. One of the firefighters who'd been injured was an old friend of Jack's sister.

But he'd wanted to be a firefighter his whole life—had worked hard to achieve his goal, to follow in his father's footsteps—and Seaport had an all-volunteer fire department. In the city, he was paid to do what he loved. In Seaport, he'd have to choose a different career, only work as a firefighter when needed and when he could get away from work if called.

A commotion from the hallway halted him midthought. Thankfully, or he'd wind up living back in Seaport, in a little house with a big yard, a white picket fence and a puppy. And maybe a few kids, all with big blue eyes and blond curls like their mother. *Whoa!* He shot to his feet. Where on earth had that thought come from? He shook his head, ridding himself of a vision that was all too appealing. If he ever did settle down in that little house, it would most definitely not be with a woman who already had a child. He'd traveled that path once before and had no intention of doing so again.

Ava strode through the waiting room door with Mischief in her arms, head resting on Ava's shoulder, arms hanging at her sides, apparently sleeping. Funny how innocent she looked in sleep without that spunky fire in her eyes.

Several men jumped up and offered Ava their seats, but she waved them off with a thank-you and walked directly to Jack.

His heart soared, and he opened his arms to her.

After only a moment of hesitation, she leaned into him.

He pulled her into his embrace, tucking Mischief between them, careful not to wake her. He dropped a quick kiss on top of Ava's head an instant before she stepped back and wiped the tears from her cheeks. She tilted her head to look up at him, and his heart broke at the pain in her eyes. This couldn't be easy for her, had to bring back painful memories. He fought the growing desire to pull her into his arms and shelter her. There was no way to save her from her own memories. He'd probably only make it harder for her.

He shoved his hands into his pockets.

"What happened?" A tremor ran through her as her gaze raked over him. "Are you hurt?"

He shook his head quickly. "No, no. I'm fine."

"Earl?"

"We haven't heard anything yet, but he did regain consciousness in the ambulance, so I think that's good." He swiped a still-trembling hand through his hair.

"Where's Serena?"

"I believe she's in the chapel with her kids and Father Walter."

Ava nodded, a concerned frown marring her features. "Is something wrong?"

"Uh…" What could he say, that he was trying to choke down the sudden desire to buy a home in Seaport and have a houseful of children? That he'd spent the last few hours reliving the pain of Carrie leaving him and taking Matthew with her? "I'm good."

But he wasn't. Not really. He was supposed to stay in Seaport for six months. That's it. Then he was going back to the city and resuming his life. Alone. The thought suddenly didn't appeal quite as much as it once had. But what else could he do? "Did you talk to the police?"

She lowered her gaze and shook her head, but not before he saw the instant of terror flash in her eyes.

"Did something happen?"

She cradled her little girl even closer to her, looked around and lowered her voice. "He called from right across the street, stood there staring at me, daring me to tell the police everything, and I caved."

"Okay, all right." He couldn't blame her. The woman was clearly terrified, had already lost her husband and was trying desperately to keep her child safe. He stroked a hand over Missy's silky hair. "We'll figure something out."

"No, you don't under—"

"Mama?" Mischief lifted her head from Ava's shoulder. "Fireman Jack?"

Ava's breath hitched.

"Yes, honey, it's fine. Everything's okay." He led Ava downstairs to a quiet section of the lobby where a small cafeteria and gift shop stood. "Can I get you anything? Something to drink?"

Ava shook her head, tears streaming down her cheeks.

The last thing Jack needed in the midst of his current turmoil was a complication like Ava and her daughter. While he'd never get involved with the fragile woman romantically, despite his ridiculous impulses, probably brought on by all the stress, it was clear she needed help. At the very least, a friend, someone she could confide in.

Mischief frowned at her mother. "Mama?"

"Here, why don't you come to me for a minute and let your mom sit and rest." When he opened his arms for her, she flung herself into them, and his heart stuttered.

Ava sat down hard on one of the plastic chairs.

"Come on. Why don't we see what they have in the gift shop?"

"Yay." Mischief clapped her hands together, instantly forgetting there was anything strange going on, in the way only the innocence of childhood would allow.

Jack walked into the gift shop with her in his arms but kept a watchful eye on Ava and anyone walking through or lingering in the lobby.

"That one." She pointed at a big, fluffy, black puppy with ears that stood straight up. "Mama says no puppy."

"Oh, she does, huh?" He lowered her to the floor, and she ran to it.

"Yup, not 'til I'm big." When she reached into the open box to hug the animal, it barked. Not the cute little yip you'd expect from a toy puppy, but a deep, ferocious bark worthy of a full-grown Rottweiler. She giggled wildly, and he couldn't resist the sheer joy radiating from her.

Jack laughed. "Are you sure that's the one you want?"

"Yup. I sure." She hugged the pup tight, and it growled as if in warning. "I love Puppy."

"Okay. Puppy it is, then." He was pretty sure Ava would be okay with a puppy that wasn't real. At least, he hoped so, because there was no way he was disappointing Mischief.

"Yay!" She clutched the dog to her, box and all, and the dog growled and barked again…and again…and again. Uh-oh.

"But you have to take real good care of him." Maybe it would be practice for when Ava crumbled and gave in to Missy's demands for a real puppy. If Ava could get past her current situation, he had a feeling Mischief could talk her mom into just about anything with one pleading look from those big blue eyes. He'd sure have a hard time saying no to her.

Jack took Missy's hand and turned, only to find Ava standing there glaring at him.

"Uh…" What could he say? Nothing, so he went with what he hoped was a charming smile. "Mischief wants Puppy."

Missy held the dog up to show Ava, squeezing away to make him growl and bark, finding joy in the midst of chaos as only a child could.

Ava lifted a brow toward the dog, but a smile played

at the corners of her mouth. "You obviously don't have kids."

"What can I say?" He winked at Mischief and laid a hand gently on Ava's back then guided her through the narrow shop's aisles as they moved toward the register. "She loves Puppy."

"Uh-huh." Though she finally smiled, her eyes remained guarded, wary, as her gaze skittered around the shop and across the lobby.

A niggle of fear crept up his spine, and he shifted to put himself between Ava and Mischief and the gift shop's open doorway while he paid for the new puppy. Once done, he checked the lobby before leading them to a small seating area situated away from any windows. Before he could ask Ava what she wanted to do, his phone rang, and he glanced at the caller ID. "I have to get this."

Ava nodded and sat directly behind Missy, who knelt on the floor and propped Puppy on a low table. She fished a small brush out of Puppy's box and started to tame his fluff.

Keeping watch over them, Jack prayed for good news as he answered. "Hey, Pat, what's up?"

"Hey, man, I didn't know where you disappeared to, but I wanted to let you know Big Earl's going to be fine."

Jack's breath shot out in a whoosh of relief. "Oh, thank God."

"He's got a mild concussion," Pat laughed, "but he's already giving everyone a hard time about staying overnight for observation. Looks like that hard head of his finally came in handy."

Jack grinned and gave Ava a thumbs-up sign.

Her eyes closed as she nodded and laid her head back against the seat. A fraction of a second later, she lurched upright and looked around.

"Jack?" Pat's tone pulled him back to the conversation.

"Oh, sorry, so what's happening? Is he going to stay? Can we see him yet?"

"They're only letting family in right now, but I don't think they're going to be able to keep him for long. He's already arguing in favor of going home, says he wants to stop by the firehouse then sleep in his own bed. Serena seems to be caving. To be honest, I think she just wants to get the kids home and put the whole thing behind them."

"I don't blame her."

"Nah, me neither."

"All right. I'll be back up in a few minutes, I just came down to the gift shop to entertain Mischief for a few minutes. Is there any other word?"

Pat paused for a minute, and when he spoke again, he kept his voice low. "The fire was deliberately set, and the arsonist didn't even bother to try to cover it up."

His gaze shot to Ava. What were the chances they had a second arsonist on the loose at the same time her attacker showed up in town? Slim to none.

"Thanks, Pat. Did you find out anything else?"

"Not yet, but I'll let you know if there's news about the others."

"Thanks, man." Jack hung up and stuffed his phone into his pocket, then put a hand on Ava's shoulder. "Big Earl's okay. He wants to stop by the firehouse and then go home with Serena and the kids. I'm sorry, Ava, but they've determined the fire was deliberately set."

Ava stared straight ahead and didn't respond, and he could read her intention as plainly as if she were already running out the door. And if Jack could see it in her eyes, so could anyone else who might be watching her.

SEVEN

"Ava?" Jack's voice pulled her from the precipice of a full-blown panic attack.

She choked back a sob.

"Are you all right?" His frown held concern and… something more. Affection, maybe? And fear, but not the kind of terror she felt at the thought of a killer, something different, more subtle. Could she blame him really, condemn him for being afraid to get involved in any way with a woman who had a stalker after her who'd already killed, attempted to kill and injured with no regard for human life?

She had to get out of there, needed air, needed space, needed time to think. Her stalker wouldn't allow any of it. She lurched to her feet, knocking her bag onto the floor. "I can't do this."

"It's all right, Ava. Pat said Earl's going to be fine. Serena's with him now." Jack's frown deepened as he bent to retrieve her bag and his gaze caught on the other bag stuffed inside it, then shot to Ava. He held her gaze as he handed it to her but didn't comment on it, though he had to know what it meant. Or maybe he didn't. "Do you want me to take you to her?"

Her relief was short-lived as she stared into Jack's eyes. "No. You don't understand. I can't do this, Jack."

"Do what?" He gripped her arm as if to steady her, then tried to guide her toward a chair. "Here, let me keep an eye on Missy for a minute so you can calm down."

"No. I have to go." There was no way she could go through losing someone else she—she stared deep into Jack's dark eyes—someone she could come to love. "I can't do this, Jack. Any of it. I'm sorry, but it's just not going to work. Please… I have to go."

"Ava, please, don't leave." He laid a hand on her arm, but she shook it off, couldn't have him touching her, couldn't stand to look into his eyes and see the hope reflected there—hope she couldn't manage to cling to, along with the hesitance she understood all too well.

"Thank you, Jack, for everything." She collected Puppy and put him back into his box with his belongings, despite Missy's whine of protest. "We have to go, honey."

"Can Puppy come?"

What could she say? She didn't want to admit anything in front of Jack about not going home, but she also wouldn't lie to Missy. So she took the coward's way out and ignored the question.

With her bag over her shoulder, Puppy's box clutched against her, and Missy's hand in hers, she avoided Jack's gaze. "I'll see you soon."

"Will you?"

Who knew? Maybe. Someday. But right now, she had to get Missy to safety. With no clear idea of where to go or what to do next, she started across the lobby, clutching Missy close, fully aware of the target on her back. No way she could run right now, encumbered not only by Puppy's box, but by the fears that continued to plague her. Was her attacker watching her? She had to assume he was. She resisted the urge to quicken her pace as she strode through the automatic doors into the dark parking lot, then kept to the little puddles of light cast by a row of dim streetlights. She didn't dare glance over her shoulder, knowing full well Jack would be standing there, hands in his pockets, watching across the lot to be sure she made it safely to the car. She could feel the weight of his gaze and all its implications practically suffocating her.

While she didn't blame herself for Liam's death, she would certainly bear responsibility if another firefighter was killed. She couldn't live with that. Whether it was Big Earl, who she'd come to care for, Jack, who was obviously a good man, or a total stranger, like the two firefighters currently fighting for their lives because she lacked the courage to do what needed to be done to take down Liam's killer.

Her footsteps echoed across the lot, and she tried to listen past them for any others. It was time stop home. Only for a few minutes. Maybe her stalker would think she'd tucked in for the night and go back to whatever hole he was hiding in until morning, and she could slip past him. Not likely, but she had to at least try to find what he was looking for. If she could just get him what he wanted, maybe he'd keep his word and leave everyone else alone. She had no illusions about her own safety. If she couldn't get out of town, she was as good as dead. Unless she could trade whatever evidence he wanted for her and Missy's lives.

She'd let Missy sleep for a little bit while she pulled

all of Liam's things back out of the closet and once again searched his belongings. She'd placated herself these past years with the fact that he'd either turned over any evidence he'd had or it had burned up in the house fire she'd fled. But she realized now she'd been lying to herself. He wouldn't have packed a flight bag then hidden something as important as evidence in the house. He'd have either had it with him or secreted it in the bag, and the more she thought about it, the more sense it made he'd have left it behind if he didn't fully trust whomever he was meeting with that day.

There must be something, some way for her to find what the attacker was looking for. But what if she found something incriminating? Could she really turn it over to the man who killed her husband and hope he'd go away, saving her daughter's life? No. Ignoring the problem for four years was one thing, but handing a killer—her husband's killer—a way out was something else entirely.

She'd have to do the right thing and hand it over to the authorities and pray they could catch the killer before he could get to Missy. Maybe they'd put them in witness protection, let her start a new life somewhere else where she wouldn't have to look over her shoulder constantly, since she had no idea how many people were involved and would never feel fully confident they'd caught them all.

Or, she could just forget everything and go on the run with her daughter, bury her head in the sand as she had since Liam's death.

But she'd built a life in Seaport, wanted to buy a business, made friends, belonged to a church and volunteered at the hospital. Did she really want to give all that up? Whether she ran herself or asked for police protection, the end result would be the same. She'd have to leave Seaport. And she would do it, if only for herself, but didn't Missy deserve a better life than moving from town to town, never forming any kind of close relationships?

When they reached the car, she held her breath long enough to get Missy strapped into her seat and run around to the driver's side, and she didn't take another full breath until she'd pulled out of the lot. She kept her eye on the rearview mirror, even though she didn't expect anyone to show up right on her bumper. Her attacker was too savvy for that. He'd watch from a distance, stalk her, bide his time while he waited to see if she'd do what he'd demanded.

At least now she knew what she was looking for. And a flash drive was small enough for Liam to have hidden in his belongings without her having found it. If it was there, though, she'd find it now. Then she'd call the police. Or maybe she'd call Jack and ask him to contact his friend Gabe, who he seemed to trust. After all, the chances of a police officer in Seaport having any connection to a firehouse in Florida were extremely slim.

She probably should have asked Jack to come with her, probably would have if she could just make a decision on whether she was going to stick around or run. With Jack around, running became less of an option. Besides, she'd be in and out in a few minutes, five tops. And she couldn't stand the thought of having anyone else hurt because of her. Not after Earl.

She thought briefly of turning around, bringing Missy back to the hospital and leaving her with Jack or Serena. But how could she? Serena's husband was in the hospital, injured because of Ava. What if he took a turn for the worse? It wasn't fair to ask her to take on the responsibility of a three-year-old right now. And as far as Jack… He seemed like a really nice guy, but it didn't change the fact she hadn't known him long enough to leave Missy with him. She hadn't really known anyone long enough to trust they'd risk their lives to save her like Ava would. And what if Ava got the opportunity to run? She'd never leave Missy. No, Missy had to stay with her.

She searched for calm as she drove, reached out to God to ask for help, to beg Him to protect Missy and, for the first time, to help her find Liam's killer. "I trust You, God. I'm trying to follow the path You've laid out for me, but I can't do it alone."

An image of Jack—his warm smile, his comforting embrace—popped unbidden into her head. Other visions flashed to her: Serena laughing, Big Earl cradling Missy, a packed hospital waiting room where an entire community huddled together praying for good news. Had God provided her support all along? Had He led her to this moment, to this community, to these people in an effort to help her? Had she been the one to turn away from His efforts, to hide from the truth?

She couldn't be sure, but she did know she was done running. It was time to fight back.

After pulling into the garage, she debated whether or not to close the door. If she did, it would mean extra seconds waiting for the garage door to go up if she had to get out fast. If not, someone could easily sneak in and break through the connecting door from the garage to the house or hide in her car. Plus, she wanted her stalker to have the illusion she'd hidden away, at least until morning. She hit the remote and waited while the door slid down behind her. If need be, she could probably just floor it and back right through to escape.

She ran around and took Missy out of the seat where she'd dozed off.

"Puppy." She reached out for the box.

Not wanting to argue with her and risk waking her further, Ava grabbed Puppy from his box, then left everything else where it was on the back seat. They wouldn't be at the house for long.

After laying Missy and Puppy on the couch, Ava returned to the car and slid the key back into the ignition. At the first sign of trouble, she could just snatch Missy up and run. She grabbed a water bottle and a knife on her way through the kitchen and set them on the living room floor. Ten minutes. She checked the time on her cell phone. She'd give herself ten minutes to go through Liam's things, gather anything of importance to take with her and get out.

Tucking her cell phone into the pocket of her jeans, she returned to the foyer and opened the small coat closet where she kept Liam's things. A rush of nostalgia threatened to overwhelm her, but she shoved it aside and scooped up the small stacks of clothing off the shelf and dumped them on the living room floor, then returned for the two pairs of shoes, a jacket and a sweatshirt.

With everything in a heap on the floor, and the knife within range, Ava knelt next to the couch, right by Missy's side, and started searching quickly but methodically. She felt through every pocket, ran her hands over every inch of fabric, checked every bump or bulge or seam that seemed out of place.

"Come on, Liam. Help me out here." A thud brought

her up short. She paused and clutched his favorite blue flannel shirt against her chest, staring at the small address book that had just fallen out of the pocket. "Maybe I'm going about this the wrong way. Maybe I should be asking who you would have trusted. Who would you have gone to with your suspicions, besides the police?"

She paged through the book, one name after another, all written in black ink in Liam's barely legible scribble. He'd warned her about ditching her phone if they had to run, said it wouldn't be safe to carry it, since it could be tracked by the right people. He must have backed up his contacts just in case. But nothing unusual stood out. No name had the words *suspected arsonist* scribbled next to it.

No time to read the entire book now.

She set it aside to take a better look at it later, wishing she'd hung around Florida long enough to pick up his belongings from his firehouse locker. A flash drive could have been among them. She'd probably be dead by now if she had waited. The killer had already said he went through Liam's locker, or someone working with him had. If it had been there, they'd have found it.

She went through the jacket next, taking precious time to search for hidden pockets or anything Liam might have sewn into the seams. Her frustration mounted when she found nothing. Tears tracked down her cheeks. He had to have left something. She wiped the tears that were blurring her vision. Time was just about up. She could fall apart later, after she and Missy were safe.

She picked up one of his sneakers that looked like it had never been worn. He must have bought new ones for the bag so he could continue to wear the old worn-out pair he loved so much. The memory brought a smile and a wave of grief. She pulled out the inner sole, reached inside as far as she could. Nothing. She turned the sneaker over, ran her fingers over the clean bottom. Her finger caught on one of the treads, and she examined it more closely.

A thin line ran through the tread. Her stomach quivered. She dug a nail into the thin gap and popped out a rectangular section of the sole. A key sat in the recess, along with a small folded rectangle of thick paper. She pulled them out. The key was small, not a house or a car key for sure. His locker at the firehouse, maybe? She took out the card and unfolded it. A business card from a bank in northern Florida, a few hours' drive from where they'd lived in Central Florida.

A noise from the side of the house by the garage brought her up short. It was time to go. She tucked the key and card into her pocket, then stuffed the block of rubber back into the bottom of the sneaker and tossed it onto the pile. Leaving everything where it was, Ava grabbed the knife and crept toward the kitchen. Empty. Everything appeared just as she'd left it.

There was no time to finish going through Liam's things, but at least she'd found something. As soon as she checked the garage, she'd get out of there with Missy and figure out what to do with what she'd found afterward.

She crossed the kitchen quietly, knife clutched in her sweaty hand, her grip on the slippery handle precarious. As she neared the door to the garage, she stopped and listened.

The door burst open, and two men, their faces covered with ski masks, shoved their way into the kitchen.

Ava swung the knife, but one of them easily blocked the blow. He gripped her wrist in an iron-tight hold, while the other man pried her fingers from the knife and tossed it aside.

Her heart stopped. *Missy.* She prayed fervently that Missy would wake up and run or hide.

The man holding her shoved her, hard, and she rammed her hip against the table and lost her footing as it slid aside. One leg buckled, and she went down on her knee. Stupid. She'd been stupid to return home. Stupid to think she could do the right thing, avenge Liam's death, and make a home in Seaport.

"Where is it?" the man who'd attacked her earlier demanded. "I'm not playing games anymore."

"I don't have any flash drive."

The second man disappeared into the living room where she'd left Missy sleeping on the couch. *Oh, no. God, please, look out for her. Protect her. Save her.*

"Give me your cell phone." The man grabbed her arm and yanked her to her feet. "Now."

She handed over the phone from her pocket. Better to just give it up than to have him search her and find the key.

"Hey, look at this, Ken." The second man stuck his head back into the kitchen and gestured toward the living room.

Ken shoved her forward.

She stumbled toward the living room. A flash drive. She had a flash drive in her bag in the car, used it for Missy to watch movies at the shop. If she gave it to them, would they leave her and Missy alive? Probably not. Once they had what they wanted, they'd surely kill her, especially now that she'd heard her attacker's name. Ken. It didn't ring a bell, but maybe Liam's address book would shed light on who he was.

If she made it out of there alive. She couldn't imagine Ken would let her walk away this time, and they would most definitely not leave without taking Missy. No way would she let that happen. If she could just incapacitate them long enough to get Missy and get out, she might have a chance to escape. A long shot, but she had to try.

She tripped going through the entryway, letting her attacker get closer, then turned and jammed an elbow into Ken's gut and when he doubled over followed through with another to his chin.

He gasped, and blood blossomed on his lip.

The other man grabbed a handful of her hair and yanked her head back, then shoved her to the floor and pointed at the pile of Liam's things. "I think she might be telling the truth. Looks like she was searching through her husband's belongings."

Ken used the back of his hand to wipe the blood from his mouth. "A man's belongings. That doesn't mean they belonged to her husband."

Ava tuned out the argument. Her gaze shot to the couch, which was empty. Thankful Missy was no longer there, but terrified about where she might have gone, Ava struggled to her feet. She ignored the flare of pain in her hip. Where would she go? The second man had only been gone for a moment and hadn't mentioned Missy when he returned. Had she woken and hid before that? The front door was closed and locked, not that that had stopped Missy from getting out before, but she wouldn't have been able to lock the dead bolt behind her, even if she did close the door.

"Where do you think you're going?" Ken gripped her arm, whirled her to face him, then punched her.

The blow to her jaw weakened her knees, and she dropped, smacking her head against the coffee table. Blood impeded her vision in one eye.

"What now?" the other man asked.

Ken scrolled through her phone, then threw it across the room in a fit of rage. "At least she didn't call the police this time, so start searching."

The second attacker refrained from any further argument and disappeared into the kitchen. Drawers and cabinets slammed open and closed, glass shattered and muttered curses allowed her to keep track of his whereabouts.

Ken strode from the room, his footsteps pounding through her head.

Frantic to get to Missy and get out, Ava pulled herself forward, belly crawling toward the end of the couch. Had Missy gone upstairs? A wave of nausea overtook her. Blackness encroached, tunneling her vision. Consciousness began to fade as she listened to the men ransacking the kitchen and garage, which her attacker surely would have done the first time if the sirens hadn't scared him off. But this time, she hadn't had time to call the police.

Movement from the corner of her eye caught her attention.

Missy stared at her from behind a chair in the corner of the room, gripping Puppy's paw tightly.

Ava tried to signal her to run, to hide, but she couldn't lift her arm.

Missy grabbed Ava's cell phone from the floor where Ken had thrown it and started to move toward her mother, but the sound of the intruders coming back had her gaze shooting toward the kitchen.

Fear beat at Ava, along with the overwhelming realization that danger could be anywhere at any time, that running wasn't going to save her daughter. She had to fight, had to learn to trust again. If she ever got out of this mess.

Missy caught her lower lip between her teeth, frozen in place, her eyes wide, her body trembling.

"Run, baby," Ava whispered as she dropped her head onto her arms and prayed.

Missy turned and fled up the stairs, and Ava finally lost her tentative hold on consciousness.

Jack checked his watch for the millionth time as he rushed through the firehouse door. He'd already stopped home briefly to check on his mother and make sure Isabella, who'd arrived a few hours ago, was settled. Once he checked on Big Earl—who'd stubbornly refused to stay in the hospital and even more stubbornly insisted he had to stop by the firehouse to take care of a few things on his way home—he was going to park outside Ava's house and keep watch until morning, or whenever she decided to run. He'd have to remember to grab a thermos of coffee on his way out.

"Hey, Jack." Pat Ryan slapped him on the back and hooked a thumb toward the kitchen. "Big Earl's in there."

"Thanks, Pat. Any word on how the others are doing?"

He grinned. "A-OK. Both doing well and are expected to make a full recovery."

Relief flooded him. "Thanks, man."

"You bet. I'll catch you later. Gonna go home and get some rest."

"Sure thing." Jack headed toward the kitchen. He should probably do the same, sleep for a little while, but he just couldn't get Ava out of his head. He'd already followed her home and seen her pull into the garage, then driven past twice more and seen a light on in the front window and a shadow moving around inside. Come morning, he was going to talk her into accepting help and see what he could do to get her out of danger. Until then—

"Hey, Jack, how's it going?" Big Earl started to stand.

"What are you trying to do? Get me in trouble with Serena?" Jack smiled, thrilled to see him up and around and back to his usual self. "Now sit down."

Earl dropped onto the chair and stretched, then folded his hands around a coffee mug on the table in front of him.

Jack pulled out a chair across from Earl and sat. That could have been a mistake. He was mentally and physically exhausted, and he'd still need to stay awake several more hours until daylight so he could catch Ava if she tried to leave. What he really needed was a quick shower, but he didn't dare take that much time. "So, how long before you're allowed to return to work?"

Big Earl grinned. "According to the doctors or Serena?"

Jack laughed. If Serena had her way, he'd probably never go back but retire early and stay home with her and the kids.

"Actually, I promised her I'd take a couple of days off, hang around the house, maybe take a look at her ever-growing to-do list if I feel up to it."

"I'm sure that'll make her happy." Now he had to make a decision. Talk to Earl about Ava, or keep her confidence? If he was going to talk Ava into going to the police, she'd need someone she trusted to watch Mischief. It wouldn't be fair or safe to keep her with them. But would talking to him without Ava's approval be a betrayal of her confidence? Probably. But what was more important: keeping her secret or keeping her safe? And it wouldn't be fair to ask Earl and Serena to keep Mischief without letting them know what was going on. Which, at the end of the day, was the only reason he was sitting at the firehouse rather than out in front of Ava's. As much as he wanted to check on Earl, that could have been handled with a phone call. Gauging his reaction to Jack's request could only be done in person. "There's something I need to talk to you about. It has to do with Ava…"

Earl's smile widened. "Boy, it didn't take you long to get smitten, did it?"

Heat flared in his cheeks. "That's not what I meant, I just…uh—"

The phone rang, buying him another few minutes to beat himself up over what to do.

Earl hit the speaker button, then leaned the chair back on two legs and folded his hands behind his head as he answered. "Seaport Fire and Rescue."

Jack blocked out the caller, his thoughts turning inward to Ava. The sentiment had caught him off guard, but Big Earl wasn't wrong, though smitten wasn't exactly the word he'd use to describe how he felt about Ava.

Earl's chair legs thudded back onto the floor, ripping Jack from being tortured by thoughts he wasn't yet ready to confront. "Sure. How can I help you?"

"We're calling all the firehouses in the area." A woman's voice came over the line, rushed, urgent, yet calm. "A nine-one-one call just came in from a young child. She's calling from a cell phone, and we can target the general vicinity, but we can't get the exact location. She's looking for Big Earl and Fireman Jack because there are bad men in the house and her mother is hurt. Do you know the child? Can you provide an address?"

The chair tumbled behind Jack as he jumped up and bolted for his truck.

"Jack, wait!"

Ignoring Earl's call, blood thundering in his ears, Jack ran. He fumbled the key into the ignition and slammed the truck into gear. He never should have left her alone, not even for a second. Why didn't he just camp outside her door if she didn't want to let him in? He thought he'd have time. Just a little while to see to his mother, check in on Earl and try to set up a safe haven for Missy. Foolish, and now Ava was paying for his mistake.

The tires spit gravel as he shot from the parking lot, praying he'd be in time to save them. And once he did, since he refused to contemplate any other outcome— couldn't if he was going to maintain any kind of rational thought—Ava was going to trust him, and he was going to stop whoever was tormenting her, whatever the cost. "I don't know what Your purpose is, God, but I can't help but think You put Ava here, in this town, at this time, for a reason. I believe You guided me on the path back to Seaport to help her. Please, don't let me have failed her and Mischief."

Tears blurred his vision, and he swiped at them. He didn't have time for emotion, had to think clearly. Though he'd initially panicked at the thought of someone hurting Ava and Missy—the thought Ava was already injured, or worse—he had to calm down and think.

What had the nine-one-one operator said? Ava was hurt. Missy had called, so she was okay. At least, she was at the time she'd placed the call. There were bad men in the house. Men. More than one. So, her attacker wasn't alone this time. Were they armed? Could he take on more than one armed intruder? Earl would have already called the police, so he'd just have to keep them safe long enough for backup to get there.

He skidded to a stop in front of the house, slammed the gearshift into Park even as he swung the door open, jumped out without bothering to turn off the truck and bolted for the house. The front door looked secure, garage door closed. He ran around the side of the house, trying to recall the layout.

The open garage window had fear plunging through him like a knife to the heart. He scrambled through the window without slowing down, skirted Ava's car and lunged through the open door. The kitchen was empty. As quietly as he could, though he was sure his thundering heart would give him away, he crept across the kitchen. Keeping to the side of the doorway, he peered into the living room, where Ava lay crumpled on the floor bleeding from a head wound.

He scanned the room as he ran to her, felt for a pulse. Relief squeezed his heart in a painful grip when the strong beat pounded against his fingers.

The sound of men arguing upstairs was the only

thing that could have torn him from her side without treating her.

Sirens screamed in the distance. Wait and treat Ava or confront the men?

"I'm not going in there with that dog." A man's voice echoed from the top of the stairs.

"You hear that?" The second voice held only cold calculation. "It's either the dog or the cops."

A muttered curse, followed by the sickening sound of the attacker hitting a door, wood splintering. "Where was the mutt the first time I broke in then?"

Jack grabbed the bronze shovel from a rack of tools beside the fireplace and took the stairs two at a time.

A dog barked, ferociously, again and again.

Brilliant, Missy. When this is done, I'm going to buy you a houseful of puppies.

The chaos of the dog barking, men hitting the door with their shoulders and approaching sirens masked any sound he might have made on the carpeted stairs, and he was able to get within a few feet of the men before one of them turned and spotted him, just as the door swung open beneath the other's weight.

Jack heaved the shovel and hit the man in the jaw.

He stumbled and shook his head to clear it.

Before the second man could attack, Jack swept both his feet out from under him.

The man fell, cracking his head against the stair railing.

When the first man grabbed Jack from behind, he whirled and met ice-cold gray eyes, a killer's eyes.

Unable to get any leverage to swing the shovel, he lifted his feet, jammed them against the wall and sent them both tumbling backward down the stairs. Jack grabbed the railing, stopping his descent halfway down and pulled himself to his feet, then surged back up to the hallway. When he reached the top of the stairs, the man was gone. A strobe of blue-and-red light bathed the hallway through Missy's window.

Silence from Missy's room tormented him, the dog no longer barking, the sirens no longer wailing, only his own harsh breathing as his lungs strained for air. With a firm grip on the shovel, Jack started into the room.

The masked man barreled through the doorway, catching Jack mid-body with his shoulder.

Jack's knee twisted, and he fell, losing his grip on the shovel as he tried to break his fall with two-hundred-plus pounds coming down on top of him.

Even as they landed, the man jumped up and untangled himself, then plunged down the stairway past Jack, grabbed his partner, who was just starting to stand, and ran.

The silence buzzed in Jack's head. Missy!

Wheezing from the hit to the chest, Jack lurched to his feet and with a hand on either side of the doorway, propelled himself into Missy's room. "Missy!"

He held his breath. Nothing.

"Mischief, it's Fireman Jack. Honey, are you here? It's okay to come out now, baby. The bad men are gone. I'm here to help you and your mom." He ignored the twinge in his knee and the ache in his chest and dropped to the floor, lifted the pink bed skirt and peered underneath. Nothing. "Mischief, honey? Please, answer me. It's safe now. You're safe now. I won't let anyone hurt you."

A soft whimper answered and she eased the closet door open and peeked out. "Fireman Jack?"

"Oh, Missy." He ran to her, scooped her up into his arms.

Puppy barked.

Missy nestled against him, still clinging to Puppy, and buried her head beneath his chin. "Puppy saved me."

A chill ripped through his entire body, leaving his nerves tingling. "Then Puppy gets a nice big steak for dinner."

Keeping Puppy between them, Missy threw her arms around his neck and hung on tight, sobbing uncontrollably.

Hugging her close, he limped through the doorway toward the stairs.

Someone pounded on the front door. "Police!"

Missy's head popped up, and she tightened her hold on his neck.

"It's okay, honey. I'm going to let the police in and check on your mom, but I won't put you down, okay?"

She nodded, popped her thumb into her mouth, and lowered her head against his chest and straight to his heart.

He shoved the burst of feelings aside. This was not the time to examine them. Besides, it was most likely the rush of adrenaline heightening his emotions. Mischief was a sweet child, her mother strong and loving. The wave of emotions he experienced were probably perfectly rational under the circumstances. But he hugged Mischief closer as he unlocked the door.

Thankfully, it was Gabe standing on the doorstep, saving him the trouble of having to explain who he was.

"What happened? Is everyone all right?"

Jack turned and ran to Ava, dropping to his knees at

her side as Gabe called for an ambulance. He smoothed her hair away from her face, checked her pulse again. "Ava?"

"Mama?" Missy sniffled and hugged Puppy closer, making him bark.

Ava stirred. Her eyes fluttered open. "Missy!"

"She's okay, Ava. I have her." Now he just had to talk Ava into trusting him.

EIGHT

A steady *beep, beep, beep*, muffled voices and footsteps and the smell of disinfectant jerked Ava awake. Her eyes shot open, and a sharp pain in her head squeezed them closed again just as quickly. She took a shallow breath and whispered, "Missy."

"Hey, take it easy. You're safe. You're in the hospital." Jack's hand enveloped hers instantly, a lifeline in the raging sea of chaos her life had become. "Missy's here, and she's fine. Right, Mischief?"

"Mama?"

So much love surged through her in that instant, with that one small word from such a soft, fragile voice, she thought she might drown beneath the intensity. She released Jack's hand and opened her arms.

Missy flopped onto the bed and hugged her fiercely, yanking on the IV line taped to the back of her hand. "Mama."

"I've got it." Jack jumped up to untangle her from the line.

Missy squeezed even harder, and Puppy growled and barked between them, sending a sharp stab through Ava's pounding head. She set Missy back just a little and studied every inch of her to assure herself she wasn't hurt, and she realized in that instant that she'd already known Missy was okay the moment she realized she was with Jack. And that realization came with another; she fully trusted Jack. Ignoring the pang of emotion she wasn't yet ready to deal with, she tucked Missy's curls behind her ear. "I see you brought Puppy."

"Uh-huh." She held Puppy out toward Ava and squeezed his sides, setting off a snarling, barking episode. "He's getting steak."

Ava lifted a brow toward Jack. "Oh, he is, is he? And why's that?"

Missy hugged Puppy against her and snuggled into Ava's arms. "'Cause he saved us."

"He did?" She smoothed a hand over Missy's hair and glanced at Jack, who was busily rearranging the IV line and wires from the heart monitor to keep Missy from detaching anything. "What happened?"

"How much do you remember?"

Two men broke into the house; she remembered that. Goose bumps raced up her arms, and she shivered and hugged Missy even closer, inhaling deeply the scent of her, losing herself for just a moment in the soft weight of her child clinging to her.

Jack grabbed a blanket from the closet and tucked it around Ava and Missy.

"Thank you."

"Do you need anything else? A sip of water, maybe?"

Cool water sounded amazing, but her stomach flipped over at the thought. "Not yet, but thank you."

"Just let me know if you need anything." He returned to his seat next to the bed, shifted the chair closer and laid a gentle hand on her arm.

Questions ricocheted through her mind, pounding against her skull in a dull throb. "I remember the men breaking in. They were looking for a flash drive, and I was tempted to give them one I had laying around, but I was afraid…"

He nodded as she trailed off, thankfully understanding her fear and her reticence to speak of it in front of Missy. "It's okay."

"I hit my head. I remember falling, praying Missy would run or hide." Tears poured down her cheeks.

"It's okay, Ava. She did. She hid and called nine-one-one, exactly like she was supposed to do." Tears shimmered in his eyes as he ruffled her curls. "Mischief is our little hero."

The sheer emotion behind the phrase caught her off guard.

"She sure is," Big Earl said from the doorway, giving Ava a moment to collect herself.

She kissed Missy's head. "I am so proud of you, baby."

Missy smiled up at her.

"Knock, knock." Serena nudged past him and hurried across the room. She leaned over and kissed Missy, then gripped Ava's hand. "Are you all right?"

Ava nodded. "I am, thank you. But I still don't understand how I got here."

Serena wiped the tears rolling down her cheeks with a balled tissue she held in her hand. If her puffy bloodshot eyes were any indication, these were not the first tears she'd shed tonight. "This little hero called nine-one-one and was able to get help, then she locked herself in her room, hid in the closet and squeezed Puppy here over and over again, scaring your attackers just long enough for Jack to get there and chase them off."

Hope surged through her. "Did the police catch them?"

Serena's gaze turned to Jack, then back to Ava, and she shook her head. "Missy was scared and crying, and you were hurt. Jack couldn't leave you to go after them, and the police arrived just minutes too late."

"I'm sorry," Jack said softly.

Ava reached for his hand and squeezed. "Sorry for what? You saved us."

He sucked in a deep breath and let it out slowly. "I wish I could have ended this for you tonight."

As much as she wanted them caught, wished Jack had gone after them instead of hanging around to help her, she only nodded. If he'd gone after them instead and something happened to Missy, or if Jack had gotten hurt trying to catch them... "I understand, and it's okay. You did the right thing, and I owe you mine and Missy's lives, a debt I can't ever repay. Thank you."

Blotches of red stained his cheeks, and he stood from the chair, flustered. "Here, Serena, please, sit."

She waved him off. "I'm okay, but please sit, Earl. For me."

"Fine." With a weary sigh, he sank into the seat Jack offered. "But only because I can't take any more nagging."

Serena laughed through her tears, all of the pain she'd suffered since the night before showing in the circles beneath her eyes and the fear shining in them, and Ava couldn't help but admire the woman's strength. "Honey, I don't really care why you do it, as long as you do."

Big Earl lifted a brow at Missy and pointed to his wife. "See what I have to put up with?"

Missy giggled.

"Ava…" Serena's expression turned somber as she sat beside Ava on the bed and took her hand, captured her gaze with an intensity that wouldn't allow Ava to look away. "Big Earl and I decided he should take a few days off after the incident yesterday and go out to Montauk to relax for a while. We rented a lovely house by the beach with a playground for the kids just a short walk down the road. There's even an ice cream parlor close by."

Jack moved closer and set a hand on Ava's shoulder. "I told them what I know, Ava. I hope that's okay."

Was it? She'd trusted him when she'd told him about her past, shared what had happened with Liam. Was it a betrayal for him to share that with someone else?

"I'm sorry." He squeezed her shoulder. "You were… uh…hurt and unconscious, and Serena offered to help with Missy, but I didn't want them to get involved without understanding…well… They have kids to look after too."

She reached up and covered his hand with her own. "It's okay, Jack. I understand. You did the right thing."

His shoulders sagged with relief, and he raked a hand through his already tousled hair.

Serena rubbed circles on Missy's back, her expression filled with so much love Ava almost fell apart right there. "I'd love to take Missy with us, give you a few days to recover, heal, take care of what you need to."

Missy popped her head up and looked at Serena. "Can Puppy come?"

"Are you kidding me?" She gave Puppy's head a pat. "All heroes are welcome to come."

"Can I, Mama? Please?" She stared up at Ava with those big blue eyes, pleading with her to say yes.

And she wanted to, wanted to get Missy as far away from the trouble coming for them as she could.

"No one will know to look there, Ava," Big Earl assured her. "A friend of mine rented the house in his name. There will be no trail back to you, no way to find us."

Serena pulled a baseball cap and boy's jacket from her oversized bag. "We'll just slip out, and no one will be the wiser."

No, no, no. How could she watch her child, her reason for dragging herself out of bed in the days after Liam's death, walk away with someone else? She couldn't. She didn't have the strength to let her child go, to trust someone else to care for her.

Missy sat up and cradled Ava's cheeks gently between her hands, as Ava often did with her when she wanted to make a point. "Please, Mama. I'll be a good girl. Promise."

Ava's heart shattered, and she choked back sobs and nodded.

"Yay." Missy kissed her and flung her arms around her neck. "Will you come too?"

She struggled to find her voice, prayed for the strength to hold on to her emotions for just a few minutes longer to reassure her baby. But when she opened her mouth, only a soft sob emerged.

"Hon, your mama can't come just yet, because the doctors still have to watch her." Jack sat on the bed next to Missy, patted Puppy on the head, then held her hand. "But I'll tell you what. Why don't I stay here and keep an eye on your mama until the doctor will let her go home, and then I'll bring her out to meet up with you guys, and we'll have a picnic on the beach? Would you like that?"

Her lower lip quivered, and she popped her thumb in her mouth. "Mama?"

Ava swallowed back the tears along with the lump clogging her throat. "It's okay, baby. You would be bored hanging out in the hospital with nothing to do. You go ahead with Serena and Big Earl, and I'll be there as soon as I can."

Missy launched herself into Ava's arms and clung tight.

Ava held on for dear life, inhaled deeply the scent that was uniquely Missy and squeezed her eyes closed, trapping the torrent of tears inside. "You have fun, baby."

Missy nodded against her.

She tried to tell her she knew she'd be a good girl, wanted to reassure her everything would be all right, wanted to beg for more time to spend with her, but the sooner they got Missy out of there, the safer she'd be. All she could manage was a husky "I love you" before Serena scooped her up into her arms.

"It's a bit chilly out tonight, so I brought one of the boys' old jackets and a hat for you to wear." With Big Earl fitting the cap over Missy's head, Serena tucked her curls quickly inside.

Once they were done, Earl leaned over for Ava to kiss Missy goodbye and tell her she loved her one more time. Earl smiled, but the strain showed in his eyes. "We're going to have the best time, right, Mischief?"

She nodded, though her smile was a bit tentative.

Ava tamped down every ounce of emotion coursing through her. "I can't wait to get there and hear all about it. Love you, baby."

And with that, Big Earl turned and left with her.

Serena leaned close and hugged her. "I promise you, we will protect that child with our lives. She'll be safe— you just make sure you are too."

Ava nodded, and the tears she'd so valiantly held back burst free. "I can't ever thank you enough for this."

Serena leaned back to look her in the eye, keeping a firm grip on her shoulders. "You don't need to. This is what family does."

Ava struggled for air, needed to fill her lungs, to ease the gaping hole Missy's absence and Serena's friendship had torn in her. She watched Serena hurry out after her husband and prayed with all her heart that God would protect them, watch over them, and keep them safe from harm.

And then a thought occurred, and she offered a prayer of thanks, so grateful that God had set her on the path He had, had surrounded her with people who served Him and would care for her and Missy in their hour of need. Even if she didn't understand God's plan for her, He obviously had one, if she chose to embrace it. Because it was her choice, a choice she suspected she'd already made.

Jack sat down next to her in the chair Big Earl had vacated and inched it even closer to her bedside, then simply waited until she cried herself out and gained control, seeming to know comfort wasn't what she needed just then.

He held a cup of water and steadied the straw for her

to take a sip, then set the cup aside and returned to his chair. "You okay?"

She nodded, worn out from the emotional roller coaster hurling her in a million different directions.

"The way I see it, you have two choices. You can take Missy and go on the run as soon as they release you, and most likely spend the rest of your life running, or you can make a stand, here and now, and finish this." Jack kept his hands fisted on the arms of the chair, didn't reach out to her, didn't do anything to sway her decision, and she appreciated that more than he'd ever know. "Either way, you have to trust in God to protect you. But if you stay and stand against them, you'll also have me at your side, and I will not let anyone near you again."

She wanted to say so many things, explain how difficult it was for her to trust anyone, even God sometimes, but she didn't. Nothing else mattered right now except keeping Missy safe, and the only way she could see to do that would be to catch whoever was stalking them and see justice done. "Where are my clothes?"

His eyes went wide, and his jaw dropped. His mouth opened and closed a few more times with no words coming out before Ava realized he'd misinterpreted the reason she wanted her clothes and thought she was going to run.

She grinned, and a small laugh erupted through her tears. "I'm not going to run. I just need to get something out of the pocket of my jeans."

He clamped a hand against his chest and sighed. "That's good, because I didn't have another speech prepared."

Ava sat up straighter, some of the fogginess beginning to clear. "Could I have some more water, please?"

Jack handed her the jeans then refilled her cup from the pitcher the nurse had left. When he turned, she held out the card and small key. "What's that?"

"I found it in a secret compartment in the bottom of Liam's sneaker in the flight bag."

Jack traded her the key and card for the water. He examined both, turned them over. "You think the key's to a safe deposit box at this bank?"

She sipped through the straw, taking one moment to revel in the blessedly cool water soothing her dry throat. "I do. At least, I hope it is. And I hope Liam left some proof in that box that will take these men down."

Jack was already nodding. He took out his phone and opened a search browser, then typed in the address on the card. "Well, at least it's a real bank."

Ava hadn't even thought to look into that.

"You want to go check it out?"

She set her water on the tray and scooted up straighter, stared him in the eye. "You don't have to come with me, Jack."

He smiled. He ran a finger along her jaw, let it linger, such a small gesture that meant so much. "Well, you're certainly not going anywhere without me."

"What about your mother?"

"Isabella's here. I don't have a big family, but we're very close. She'll stay with my mom until I return. Actually, she's talking about staying permanently with the kids and letting her husband deal with selling the house." He cupped her cheek.

Ava leaned into his touch, accepting the warmth and strength and comfort he offered. She nodded and tried to fight the tears prickling the backs of her lids.

The door opened, and Jaelyn, Ava's nurse, rushed in

with a smile. "Sorry to interrupt, guys, but it's time for me to check your vitals and give you your pain meds."

Jack stood and backed away from the bed, giving Jaelyn room to work and Ava space to collect herself.

Ava held out her arm for the nurse to take her blood pressure. "Do I have to take the pain meds?"

"Not if you don't want them, but the doctor okayed it if you feel like you need it. You took quite a nasty bump to the head there—you must have a killer headache."

Actually, she did, but the last thing she needed right now was her brain clouded from medication. "Thank you, but I'm okay."

Jaelyn finished up with the vitals and asked Ava if she needed anything else.

"No, I'm good."

"Just ring if you change your mind." She closed the door behind her as she left.

Jack returned to Ava and sat beside her. "So, what's next?"

"What do you mean?"

He scooted to the edge of the chair and rested his elbows on his knees, leaning close to her. "Well, you've got that card and the key Liam had hidden. Would you like to turn it over to the police and let them handle it?"

Yes. More than anything, she'd like to hand the entire situation off to the police and let them figure out what happened and take care of it, but she couldn't. Or, at least, she wouldn't. "If I hand over what little evidence I might have, and it disappears, I'm back to square one with nothing. Then Missy and I may never be safe again."

Jack was already nodding. "Okay, so we'll go down to Florida, see if this leads anywhere."

A smile tugged at her. "We?"

"You don't think I'd let you go alone, do you?" He grinned, then sobered. "But you have to promise me, once we look into this, see if he left anything down there like we suspect he did, you will go to the police with any evidence we find."

"I can agree to that, but depending on what we find, I may want to take it to the police up here rather than down in Florida."

He held out his hand.

She slid her hand into his to seal the deal. "I don't know how to thank you, Jack, how to thank any of you for helping me. Honestly, if it weren't for Missy, for wanting to keep her safe and maybe give her a better life than that of a fugitive, I'd never risk anyone else getting hurt."

Jack shifted closer, weaved his fingers between hers. "You're not risking anyone else, Ava. You're simply allowing people to choose to help you. And make no mistake, it is a choice. A choice each of us makes because we care about you and Missy. And also because we want to see Liam's killer brought to justice. He deserves that, Ava, and I already know Earl and Serena feel the same, because we discussed it."

The fact he could care about Liam, a man he'd never even met, touched her like nothing else could have, made her trust him in a way she didn't know she was still capable of. "Thank you. I'm sorry I've had such a hard time trusting you. It's not your fault but a fault within me."

"You're welcome." He brought her hand to his lips, brushed the lightest kiss over her knuckles. "I've had to deal with my own trust issues, and I completely understand it doesn't come easy after you've been betrayed, hurt so bad you feel like you've been shattered."

Ava sensed something deeper there, something he didn't want to talk about, a wistfulness she noticed in his eyes sometimes when he thought no one was looking.

"And it's okay to have a difficult time finding trust in others. Especially after all you've been through, and considering whoever Liam had trusted probably betrayed him. But you have to start to trust yourself. And you have to have faith in God. He gives power to the weak and strength to the powerless."

"Isaiah, right?" She remembered the quote, or something similar, from when she'd first turned to the Bible after some of the anger over Liam's death started to turn to grief. She'd gotten caught up on it, prayed for the power to do something about the man who'd killed him. Was Jack the answer to that prayer?

He smiled and nuzzled her cold hand against the warmth of his cheek. "You're an amazing woman, Ava. Your strength and courage humble me, and together, with God's help, we will find who did this, and we will stop them."

Jack listened to the steady beep of the heart monitor, watched the rhythm of the heart that held such strength. After they'd gone over the plan so many times he could recite it in his sleep, she'd finally dozed off, but mostly slept fitfully. As soon as the doctors released her, probably in the morning sometime, they'd grab something to eat and then leave for Florida. The sooner they got this taken care of, the sooner Ava and Mischief would be safe, and the sooner Jack could...

Could do what? Leave her and go back to New York City?

He gripped her hand tighter. Not likely. And yet, what choice did he have? None. He had to go back. He thought of Matthew, his little boy. No, not his, because Carrie had changed her mind about spending her life with him. Losing her had hurt badly enough, but losing Matthew had devastated him. He couldn't go through that again. He simply couldn't.

The door creaked open a crack, and a nurse glanced over his shoulder then slipped into the room. With a curt nod toward Jack, he started toward Ava, a syringe held ready in his hand. A mask covered most of his face, but the instant his eyes met Jack's, recognition struck: the attacker from Ava's house.

"What are you doing?" Jack was on his feet even as the man grabbed hold of Ava's IV line.

"Just time for her pain meds," he answered coolly.

"She refused pain meds." Jack moved toward him as he spoke, rounded the bed to stand between the man and the door. He had to get to him before he could inject anything into her IV.

He shrugged. "She must have changed her mind."

Keeping one eye on Jack out of the corner of his eye, the man slid the needle into the IV port.

Jack lunged, grabbed his wrist and twisted, forcing him to release his hold on the syringe.

The man swung hard, connected with Jack's jaw, staggering him. The instant Jack's hold loosened, the man ripped free of his grip and ran back to the bed.

Ava screamed.

He had to stop him. Where was the guard? Jack hooked an arm around the man's neck from behind, catching him in a choke hold and wrenching him back away from Ava.

"What's going on in—" Jaelyn stopped in the doorway.

"Where's the guard?" Jack yelled. After the police had questioned Ava, they'd left an officer to stand guard at the door.

"He's not there." Jaelyn ran to the bed and pressed the button for the nurse's station to summon help.

The man shoved backward, slamming Jack into the equipment monitoring Ava.

Afraid he'd pull something loose, Jack relaxed his hold, and the guy spun into him, landing a solid blow to the side of Jack's head, then once again lunged toward the bed.

After untangling himself from a mess of tubes and wires, Jack tackled the guy from behind.

He landed flat on the floor, smacking his head against the corner of a cabinet, and lay still.

Jack scrambled to his feet. "Is anyone hurt?"

Jaelyn looked up from where she'd unhooked Ava from the IV and heart monitor and shook her head. "We're okay. Ava's just shaken."

With Ava's safety uppermost in his mind, Jack yanked the closet door open, grabbed her clothes and shoved them at her, then ushered them both toward the bathroom. "Get Ava in the bathroom and dressed. Keep the door shut until I tell you."

When he turned around, the guy was already on his feet and had the window open.

"Hey!"

He lunged out, hung from the second-story window for an instant then let go.

Jack crossed the room in three steps. He had to go after him, had to catch him. He could end this here and now, and Ava and Missy would be safe. He had one leg out the window, was straddling the sill, when a car fishtailed around the corner. The door swung open as the car skidded, and the attacker half ran, half limped the last few feet and dove in. The car took off without even waiting for the door to swing shut, and it was too dark for Jack to get a look at the license plate or any other identifying characteristics other than a dark sedan. Frustration made him want to scream. Instead, he swung himself back into the room.

Ava stood with Jaelyn and several other nurses, along with hospital security. She was shaking something awful.

"Where's the officer who was at the door?" Jack asked.

"We found in him in the supply closet across the hall, unconscious but alive," one of the nurses said.

Gabe ran into the room. "Jack, we got a nine-one-one call about a fight in here. What happened?"

Jack took him aside, away from the chaos, and explained what happened. "I'm going to take Ava out of here. They just admitted her for observation, anyway, and I can do that myself. I think she'll be safer that way."

Gabe shook his head. "I don't disagree, but I can't tell you to sign her out against medical advice."

"Let's be honest, Gabe. Everyone will be a lot safer if I can get her out of here." And that's what it all boiled down to, keeping as many people as possible safe. "But I want to go now, before her attackers get a chance to regroup and come at her again."

Gabe looked around at the mess littering the floor and nodded. "Go, I'll take care of everything else."

After giving Gabe a quick rundown of events, Jack took Ava's arm. "Come on."

She started to open her mouth, then took one look into his eyes and followed without a word.

He'd seen which way the car had pulled out, had told Gabe which direction they'd gone, and his truck was parked on the other side of the hospital. With a tight hold on Ava's elbow, Jack scanned the area as they crossed the dark lot. When she tried to pick up the pace, he held her back. "Just take your time. A couple strolling to their car is a lot less likely to draw attention than two people running at this time of night."

Ava nodded, her expression blank.

Hopefully, he was doing the right thing by removing her from the situation. He didn't even have any equipment with him to keep track of her vitals. He could stop home, or even at the firehouse, and pick up what he needed, but if there was even the remotest possibility they were followed out of the hospital parking lot, there was no way he wanted to bring danger to anyone else.

NINE

Sunrise Highway on eastern Long Island was empty so early in the morning, though they'd no doubt run into traffic soon enough as they should hit the Belt Parkway just in time for the morning rush hour. The hum of the tires against the pavement and Jack's soft breathing were the only sounds.

"I understand why we shouldn't get a flight to Florida, since you have to show ID. Without knowing who's involved and what kind of information they might be able to get their hands on, they could possibly find out I'm on a flight." A chill raced through her at the memory of her attacker saying he'd found her through a facial recognition program, which it didn't seem your average, everyday criminal would have access to. The thought of them bringing down an entire aircraft full of people just to get at her made her blood run cold. When she'd run the idea past Jack, he hadn't argued, simply said he wouldn't put it past the man if the ice-cold rage in his eyes was any indication. "But you're sure we shouldn't just get a train into Penn Station and hop on Amtrak to go down?"

Jack seemed to contemplate the idea for the umpteen

millionth time in the fifteen minutes since they'd left the hospital parking lot. Neither of them had had any kind of decent sleep over the past two nights, and the drive south would take the better part of twenty hours. At least on the train they could relax and close their eyes, even if they couldn't sleep. "Yeah, I'm sure. We wouldn't need ID for the Long Island Rail Road train into Penn, but I'm pretty sure we'd have to show it for the Amtrak tickets to Florida. If we switch off, one of us sleeping while the other drives, and we only stop for gas, we should be able to make northern Florida in between sixteen and eighteen hours. Amtrak would take longer, plus we'd have to rent a car and show ID to pick it up when we got there. I'd prefer to leave as little of a trail as possible."

She didn't blame him there. There was a certain amount of safety in anonymity. "We'll have to sleep before we can drive back."

He gave a noncommittal shrug. "We'll see what happens. Let's just worry about getting there first."

She lifted her head from the seat and studied his profile, the strong set of his jaw, the compassion in his eyes when he turned to look at her, a combination that was hard to resist.

"She'll be okay, Ava. You've already spoken to Serena twice, and Big Earl assured me everything is fine. Some of the guys from the firehouse are even taking turns working security at the house they rented."

She nodded, unable to force words past the lump in her throat. Not that he was wrong; he wasn't, but knowing that didn't make it any easier to leave Missy.

"So, I was thinking…" Jack hesitated.

Uh-oh, what now? She regretted the thought the instant it surfaced. She just couldn't take anything else at the moment.

"When this is all over, how would you feel about me taking Missy to pick out a puppy?"

Caught off guard, Ava couldn't help but laugh. "Don't even tell me you two are going to gang up on me now."

He shot her a wicked grin and waggled his eyebrows. "I figure there's no way you can say no to both of us."

When this is over, he'd said, not *if.* And his confidence was almost her undoing. The fact that he had every intention of standing with her, of seeing Liam's killer brought to justice, of keeping her and Missy safe was more than she ever could have expected. The idea that maybe he'd hang around afterward, if only for a little while, gave her the slightest bit of hope they'd actually make it through this mess. "We'll see."

"I guess that's better than a no." His grin widened. "Besides, Mischief let me in on a little secret…"

"Oh? And what's that?"

He lowered his voice to a stage whisper and leaned toward her. "*We'll see* is secret code for yes."

Some of the tension seeped out of her, and she relaxed against the seat, settling in for the four-or-so-hour stretch before they'd need to stop for gas, hopefully at the last exit on the Jersey Turnpike. "Oh, it is, is it?"

"That's what Mischief says, and who am I to argue? She knows you best…" He turned his gaze on her, his expression intense. "For now."

Oh, boy. She was not ready for that, nor for the instant flare of joy that accompanied the thought. She turned her gaze out the side window, and caught headlights in the side-view mirror, still a distance back, but maintaining a steady pace in the same lane as them. She stiffened.

He glanced in the rearview mirror. "I already saw it. He's been behind us for a while now. I don't know yet if it's just an innocent person going in to work who happens to be driving the same speed as us, or if he's biding his time until there are no other vehicles in sight where someone could call nine-one-one to try to take us out."

Since there was nothing to say, she simply kept her eye on the side-view mirror and held her breath.

"So…" Jack adjusted the rearview mirror, his gaze constantly skipping between it and the road ahead. "What do you do when you're not busy trying to keep Mischief out of trouble?"

"I'm always trying to keep Mischief out of trouble." She shot him a grin so he'd know she was teasing, then she tried to give the thought serious attention. "Honestly, I don't know. I like to read. A lot. Other than that, I don't do much but work and take care of the house and Missy."

She was doing what she loved most. "What about you? What do you like to do?"

"Nope, sorry, you're not getting off that easy." He reached out a hand, tentatively weaved his fingers with hers and rested their clasped hands on the console between them then smiled. "I want to get to know you better, know something about what your life is like when you're not running from a killer."

Her heart rate kicked up a notch, and it had nothing to do with whomever he kept studying in the rearview mirror. "I enjoy the shop, chatting with customers, creating arrangements. I love my house, including cleaning and especially yard work. I'd even been thinking lately of buying my own house, maybe the one we've been living in if the landlord would agree to sell. I've saved some of the money Liam had tucked away in the flight bag and added to it for a down payment, but I have to be on the books to get a mortgage. If I could ever manage that, I had visions of planting a garden, maybe putting in a small koi pond. And Missy is the light of my life. I'm determined to spend every single second with her. I don't want to look back when she's grown and realize I've missed anything."

She tilted her head and studied him, wondering if he was bored. He didn't seem to be, even though he was fully focused on the road, but a small smile made his dark eyes shine. "Your turn now. What do you do for fun?"

His gaze intensified but only for a second. He shrugged. "Pretty much anything. I love the outdoors, hiking, bike riding, and especially the beach."

"Don't you miss the beach when you're in the city?" She'd only been living on Long Island for six months but when she thought of fleeing, the beach was one of the things she expected to miss most. Missing the Florida beaches was one of the reasons she'd been drawn to Long Island in the first place. Nothing like being able to find a beach no matter what direction you headed.

"Yes and no. I missed being able to just go surfing or scuba diving anytime I felt like it, but it's not that far to drive out on a weekend. And I visit my mother a lot, so…" He shrugged. "It usually works out. Do you have family around here?"

Pain lanced her heart. Such a normal question, but even after all these years and the pain of losing her other half, the ache in her heart hadn't lessened.

"No." Would it seem rude to just leave it at that? She tried to gauge his reaction, to see if he expected more of an answer. He waited patiently. That was one thing she'd noticed about Jack. He appeared to have all the patience in the world. And he didn't ever push or seem to have any expectations. She had no doubt if she left it at that one word, he'd accept it and move on. "My parents and my younger brother, Tommy, were killed in an accident when I was eighteen."

He squeezed her hand. "I'm so sorry."

She nodded and lowered her gaze, not wanting to elaborate. It was the first she'd spoken of the incident since she'd told Liam. He'd been such a good listener. She had a feeling Jack would be too. Safer to move on before she got too comfortable and started sharing things better left alone.

Tears pricked the backs of her eyes. What was she doing? She should never have agreed to go anywhere with him, to allow him to put himself in danger for her. She'd accepted the fact she was meant to be alone. After her parents and brother, she'd taken a chance on loving Liam. And look how that had ended. Why was God tempting her again? If this was some kind of test, she was obviously failing miserably. A tear tipped over and slid down her cheek.

"Anyway." She sucked in a deep, shaky breath and tried to rein in her emotions. This wasn't fair to him. It wasn't fair to let him risk everything thinking there might be the chance for something more between them. "I like you, Jack. You seem like a really nice guy, and I am so grateful to you for everything you're doing to help me, to help Missy, but I can't go through being hurt again. Please understand. It's nothing personal. I don't do casual flings, and I can't deal with another relationship. I'm really sorry."

"It's okay, Ava." He lifted her hand to his mouth and brushed his lips lightly over her knuckles. "I understand, and to be honest, I'm not looking for anything more either, but I'd be thrilled to consider you and Mischief friends."

She choked back a sob and nodded, grateful he understood. She was happier than she'd like to admit that he wouldn't walk out of her life for good because she could never offer him any more than friendship.

He tilted his head and contemplated her before speaking softly. "I was a young boy, not much older than Missy, when my father died, but I still remember the day the other firefighters came to the house. My mother screamed and collapsed on the foyer floor."

Ava's heart lurched, knowing how his mother would have suffered, aching for the pain the child must have suffered. What would that loss have been like for him? How would Missy have felt if she'd been old enough to understand the loss of her father, if she had known him and missed him?

He paused, staring out the windshield, then flipped on the wipers as a slow but steady rain started. "It's the only time I can ever remember seeing her like that. After that, she picked herself up and did what needed to be done to take care of us. She worked two jobs to support us at times, but she always made time for us, was always there when we needed her. Don't get me wrong, she was the best mother anyone could have asked for, but she was different after he died. There was a sadness about her, especially at times when she thought no one was looking."

"Did she ever meet anyone else?"

"No. Never even dated. I think she buried a part of herself with my dad." He looked like he wanted to say something more, but then he shook his head, glanced in the rearview mirror and frowned.

But Ava understood. She could completely get why Miss Jenny wouldn't have moved on. The thought of it was too painful. "I don't think it's something you can understand, the not being able to get past the grief, unless you've been married and lost your spouse."

"I've never lost a spouse, not to death, anyway, but I was married…"

The admission came as a shock, though she couldn't say why.

"And I did lose her when she walked out on me with the boy I viewed as a son." His jaw clenched tight, and he made a visible effort to relax it. "She cheated on me when we were engaged, and I forgave her, offered to raise the baby as my own. I loved that boy with everything in me, and she walked out and took him away to live with his real father."

"Oh, no, Jack, I'm so sorry. I don't know what to say." And the pain was etched into every sharp angle of his features so she knew it was something he'd never get over, suspected it was the reason he wasn't looking for any kind of serious relationship. She couldn't blame him, really. Losing those you loved was difficult and painful enough when it was a tragedy that took a loved one from you, but to lose a child he so obviously cared deeply for because a woman he should have been able to trust walked out with him had to leave its own scars.

"Nothing to say. It was a choice I made to step aside

and let Matthew have a good life with his mother and father, without the complication I'd present."

She rubbed her thumb back and forth over his hand still clasped in hers, her heart aching at the thought of the agony it must have caused him to let his little boy go. "Loving someone is never a complication, Jack."

"With my ex it would have been. Anyway…" He smiled, though the sadness in his eyes still remained. "I can't change the past, and if I could, I wouldn't. At least I had a little while with Matthew, and who knows, when he's older, maybe things will be different."

But she could read the disappointment even as he made the statement; he knew in his heart it wouldn't be. She wanted to reach out to him, wanted to tell him it would be all right, but it was a pain he would always carry with him, so she just held his hand, offering what little comfort she could.

"Look, Ava, my life is in a bit of upheaval right now, and I wasn't looking for a relationship. But I like you— and Missy—and I'd enjoy the chance to get to know you better. Just friends, nothing more."

She smiled back through her tears and nodded. "That would be great."

"Good, now, as your friend, I'm going to have to ask you to trust me." He hit the turn signal and slowed as they approached an exit. "And I know that doesn't come any easier for you than it does for me."

She braced for trouble. "What's wrong?"

"Nothing, maybe…" He frowned again in the mirror. "But the car behind us has been pacing us since we got on the highway out east. I can't leave him back there, can't take a chance it's your attacker following us, especially if he can phone ahead to a second attacker who could lie in wait. Besides, I don't really want them to figure out we're headed down to Florida, so I'm going to get off here."

"Are you going to try to lose him?" She started to turn and look out the back window, but his hold on her hand tightened.

"No, keep an eye on him in the mirror. I don't want to tip him that I know he's there." He took the exit ramp slow enough for her to keep the car in sight.

"He's following."

Jack only nodded and released her hand to grip the wheel with both hands.

"What are you going to do?"

"First, I'm going to hope he doesn't know the area. There's a police station about two miles off the exit. If we can get close before he makes a move, they might be able to catch him." He grabbed his cell phone from the cup holder and dialed nine-one-one.

Jack set the phone to the Bluetooth to free up both hands, then carefully explained to the nine-one-one operator that they were being followed and that several attempts had already been made on Ava's life, then asked for a police cruiser to intercept the car behind them.

The operator remained on the line with him while he rounded a corner and slowed down. God willing, this would end here and now. As soon as the police cruiser could get there and come up behind them then pull the man over, they'd have him. If nothing else, it would buy them the time they needed to get down to Florida and finally make sense of what was going on.

But the police hadn't arrived yet, and he was too close to the station. One more right turn and it would come into sight. If the guy panicked and took off, they'd lose their chance. Jack made a left and relayed his position to the operator. He picked up speed as they headed through an area rife with abandoned warehouses and apartment buildings. Pretty much the worst place they could have ended up.

The driver behind him accelerated.

"Hold on."

Ava braced her hands against the dashboard as Jack hit the gas.

Ignoring a stop sign, he whipped around a corner too fast, and the back end skidded out. He fought the wheel for control.

The impact came out of nowhere, as a second vehicle broadsided his side of the car.

He relayed their position to the operator even as he hit the brakes, then turned his mind to getting out of this mess because the cavalry was probably not going to arrive in time. The nine-one-one operator's frantic pleas for an update barely registered as he leaned across Ava and shoved her door open. "Go. Now."

Ava half jumped, half tumbled out the door, landing on one knee on the pavement.

Jack scrambled out behind her, then hooked a hand beneath her armpit and yanked her up.

A man slid over the back of the car and lifted a hand to swing.

"Run." Jack shoved Ava ahead, used his right arm to block the blow, then plowed his fist into the man's gut. When the guy doubled over, he followed through with a cross to the jaw. His legs buckled, and Jack hit him again, laying him out flat.

The sound of a gunshot destroyed any sense of safety. *Ava.*

Crouching low, with his back pressed against the car beside the back tire, Jack sucked in air as quietly as he could while he listened for any sound of pursuit. Between his heavy breathing and his own heartbeat pounding a steady staccato in his head, he couldn't make out anything.

Where had Ava gone? He crept toward the front of the car, careful to keep his head low. He didn't dare call out, terrified Ava might answer and alert the killer to her position, if she hadn't already been shot. No, he refused to believe that. He'd pushed her forward, toward the crumbling remains of what had once been a three-story apartment building. Had she gone in?

He sucked in a deep breath, then another, and shoved off, keeping his head down as he ran across the weed-choked parking lot, wincing at the loud noise the glass made crunching beneath his feet.

Sirens wailed in the distance. Great, help was finally coming, and it was interfering with his ability to hear anything.

He ducked through a hole in the side of the brick building, tripped over some of the bricks scattered across the floor, then kept his back against what was left of the wall while he waited for his eyes to adjust to the dark interior. With too many windows boarded up, the streetlights barely penetrated the blackness. Even if he dared use a light, he'd left his phone in the car. He scanned the area, making out nothing more than black blobs of shape and shadows. The scant light coming through the hole in the wall highlighted piles of litter and debris scattered across the floor. No way to move quietly in there. Now what? Wait for the police? Go back out? Search the building?

Jack stayed quiet, praying fervently the shot he'd heard hadn't hit Ava. She could be lying dead somewhere, her killer already on the run, while he stood with his back against the wall doing nothing. "Ava?"

He crouched down, trying to see as far as he could across the floor and chanced another whisper. "Ava?"

Nothing.

The sirens grew louder, almost on top of them.

From his right, a dark figure burst from the shadows and hurled himself through a broken window.

Jack dove back through the gap in the wall after him.

As the guy rounded the corner of the building and disappeared, a spotlight shined right on Jack. "Freeze!"

Jack stopped and turned toward the voice, then pointed at the corner the man had disappeared around. "He's getting—"

"Hands in the air."

Jack shot his hands up. Frustration threatened to crush him. "But—"

"Keep your hands where I can see them."

As two officers moved toward him, one of their flashlights played over the man Jack had taken down, where he still lay unconscious beside the car.

Jack breathed in deeply and let his head fall back against the wall, knowing he wouldn't get to explain and find Ava until the officers were confident he posed no threat. At least they'd have one of the attackers, and maybe they'd finally get some answers.

Keeping his hands in view, Jack tried again. "I'm the

one who called nine-one-one. The woman I was with might be injured…" *Or worse.*

One of the officers kept his light trained on Jack while the other turned him toward the wall and patted him down for weapons. "Where's the woman?"

He opened his mouth to answer, to say he didn't know and couldn't bear the thought of something having happened to her, of having failed her.

"I'm here." Ava ducked out from the same hole Jack had gone in.

Ava! His breath shot out, and an ache spread across his chest as he reached for her.

She ran to him and threw herself into his arms.

"Ava. Are you all right?" He set her back, gripping her arms as he looked her over. "Are you hurt?"

"No, I'm okay, just shaken." Tears streamed down her face, reflecting the streetlights. "I went after him, tried to follow him when he rounded the building, but he jumped in a car and took off. I couldn't get the license plate number."

He pulled her against him, held on for dear life. She fit perfectly there in his arms, as if she were made to be in just that spot. He rested his chin on her head, smoothed a hand over her hair, wished he could just stay in that exact moment forever. The sudden realization that friendship might not be enough staggered him.

One of the officers cleared his throat. "Sir, ma'am, we're going to need to ask you some questions."

"Of course." Shifting so he could keep Ava beneath his arm, Jack turned to the officers.

Two others had already arrived and were bent over the unconscious assailant. An ambulance pulled into the lot.

"Can you tell me what happened?"

Jack sighed. There was no way to rush the process along, no chance they'd get out of there and back on the road until he'd answered their questions, so he did. He ran through the entire story, waited while they contacted the police in Seaport to corroborate it, watched while the guy he'd punched regained consciousness and was loaded into the ambulance without answering a single question and kept the key and bank business card to himself since Ava didn't offer the information when they questioned her.

One look at his car told him it wasn't going anywhere, so, when the police were finally done with their questions, as the sun rose higher and higher in the sky, he and Ava crossed the street from the police station to a diner while they waited for Pat Ryan to show up with a car they could borrow.

Jack cut a piece of meat lover's omelet he really didn't want, since his stomach was still raw from the fear he'd felt when he couldn't find Ava.

"I'm sorry I didn't answer when you called." Ava pushed her food around the plate too. "I was scared he'd find me."

He lowered his fork to his plate and reached across for her free hand. "You did the right thing. I wasn't even sure I should call out, wouldn't have if I hadn't heard the gunshot and been afraid he'd shot you and you might need help."

She nodded, keeping her gaze lowered.

"You need to eat something while we're held up here anyway. Once we get on the road again, I don't want to have to stop until we need gas." One positive thing, anyway, at least they wouldn't hit the Belt Parkway at rush hour now.

Ava looked up at him, tears in her eyes. "You're still going to go with me?"

"Of course I am. I already called Pat while you were talking to the police, and he's on his way with a car we can borrow for the trip."

She smiled then, and it warmed his heart in a way he couldn't begin to understand. Maybe because he'd been so afraid she'd been hurt earlier, or maybe it was just something about her that touched him in a way no one ever had before. Either way, he had no intention of letting her go anywhere on her own.

"I don't know how to thank you, Jack. There is no way I can ever tell you how grateful I am for everything you're doing for me and Missy."

"Do you really want to thank me?"

"Of course."

"Good…" He forced a grin. "Then eat some of that food so we can get out of here once Pat shows up."

"I can do that." She grinned back and took a bit of her omelet. "Mmm…this is actually really good."

He picked his fork back up and took his own advice. She was right. The omelet was delicious. "Why don't we talk about something less stressful while we eat?"

"Sure." She shrugged. "Like what?"

"For starters, I'm really dying to know how Mischief got her nickname, which, by the way, suits her incredibly well."

"I thought you said less stressful?" Ava laughed, and her eyes filled with love even as she shook her head. "It was somewhere around the third or fourth nine-one-one call. Big Earl came to rescue her when she stuck her head between the stair railings and we couldn't get her back out."

The image popped into Jack's head as if he were there, Missy stuck between the bars, tears rolling down her cheeks, Ava standing over her ready to protect her from the world, helpless that she couldn't. "That must have been scary."

"It definitely was." She sighed, set aside her fork and sipped her coffee. "But not nearly as scary as the time I left her sleeping on the couch to jump in the shower quick and came out to find the front door standing open and Missy gone, or the time I woke up at seven in the morning to find her hanging out the upstairs window. I keep—used to keep—my bedroom windows open from the top at night, and only enough to let some air in. She woke up before me one morning and saw baby birds in the nest we'd been watching in the tree right outside the window. She piled stuff on the chair by the window and managed to climb up and pull the window down enough to wiggle through. I thank God every day she got stuck halfway through."

Jack was horrified for about two seconds before laughter took over. "I'm sorry."

"I didn't sleep for about a week after that. Thankfully, she got stuck, or else…"

He shivered at the thought. "She sounds like quite a handful."

"That she is, but I wouldn't trade it for anything in the world. She's rambunctious and gets into more than her share of trouble, but she's also independent, curious and strong—all qualities that will serve her well as she grows up."

Jack simply stared at her, wondering how she could

be so amazing, could see past the trials of today to the benefits of tomorrow. "You're an incredible mother, Ava, and a fascinating woman. I can see where Missy gets her strength from."

Patches of red flared in her cheeks, and she lowered her gaze to her plate.

"Now, finish up your breakfast. Pat will be here soon, and I want to get started." He signaled the waitress for one more cup of coffee. If he was going to make it all the way to Florida without having to pull over to sleep, which he was really hoping to do, he'd need the caffeine. "We need to finish this and get back to Mischief before she drives Big Earl and Serena to their wits' end."

Ava's laughter touched him deeply. He'd been so sure he would never be interested in getting involved with a woman with a young child, never mind a woman who lived out on the Island and wouldn't want to move to the city with him. But the more time he spent with Ava and Missy, the happier he became. They just made him feel good—complete in a way he'd never felt before— despite the desperate circumstances.

His ex-wife had been a needy woman. She'd always needed someone to take care of her, to dote on her, to adore her. Truthfully, that sense of vulnerability had originally lured him more than anything else. He'd wanted to take care of her.

But Ava was different. She was independent and strong. She seemed to have her life under control, to be content, if not for the mess she was in, and even, in some ways, in spite of the mess. Yet she held him at arm's length, especially when he offered to help her. As much as he loved living in the city, and felt like he had no choice but to return, he was finding himself suddenly tempted to stay in Seaport—at least until he saw if this could go anywhere.

Whoa! Where had that thought come from? And what happened to just friends? He massaged his temples, trying to rid himself of the craziness. Falling for this woman was dangerous, and yet he couldn't seem to pull away, couldn't help but feel his whole life was in upheaval.

They say God works in mysterious ways, but this is ridiculous.

Jack finished all of his breakfast, hoping they could at least make the end of Virginia before stopping for dinner, and looked out the window. Pat had just texted he'd be there in about ten minutes.

Ava tilted her head and studied Jack. "So, what was it like growing up on Long Island?"

"It was great. Everyone knew each other, looked out for one another." Fond memories flittered through his mind: all the neighborhood kids getting together for a game of basketball, bike riding or even just hanging out in the woods with dirt bikes and quads. "Of course, that worked to my disadvantage too. One day Mr. Jenkins caught me smoking out behind his barn with his son and another boy."

"Uh-oh."

The memory brought laughter now, but it definitely hadn't been funny at the time. "He hauled me home to my mother and made me tell her what I'd been doing. Trust me, that was not a good summer. I spent every day working in the fields of his small farm."

But he'd learned a lot that summer, came to understand the importance of being responsible. Too bad it took a few more years for the lessons to actually kick in.

Ava winced. "Ouch."

"I'll say. I was so tired at the end of the day, I didn't even want to go out, never mind find trouble."

Ava smiled. "Maybe that was the idea."

Her musical laughter enveloped him. She raised a brow. "Did you get in a lot of trouble growing up?"

He thought back. At the time, he hadn't realized what the big deal was about some of the things he'd done. Only later, looking back, could he see he'd been a handful, not unlike Mischief. "Not really. More mischievous things than anything."

"Oh, like what?"

Since she seemed to be enjoying the moment, to have stepped back for just a little while from the fear that seemed to be her constant companion, he dug for a story to share. The memory he hadn't thought of in more than a decade came back and brought a smile with it. "When I was a teenager, a bunch of us used to skip out of school in the spring and go pool hopping."

"Pool hopping?"

"Yeah, we used to walk down Dune Road and try out all the pools. The mansions that line the barrier island were a perfect target for kids. Leaving them sitting empty most of the year seemed like such a waste, so we'd hop the fences and go for a swim even though half the time the water was still freezing."

"Did you ever get caught?"

"Only once." But that was all it had taken. "My mother drove me to each of the houses—some of them she had to go back to three or four times to find someone home—and made me apologize and offer to clean the pools free of charge."

"Sounds like your mother had her hands full too." Ava laughed, tears tracking down her cheeks. "She didn't tolerate much, did she?"

"No." But she'd taught him well, and he could look back and realize what had seemed like childish fun at the time was not only inappropriate and illegal but dangerous as well.

"She sounds as strict as my parents were."

As soon as he got home, he intended to give his mother a big hug and thank her for putting up with him all those years and for shaping him into the man he'd become. "I didn't appreciate it enough back then."

"No, me neither."

The waitress arrived. "Can I get you anything else?"

Jack looked at Ava, but she shook her head. "No, thank you."

When they both declined, she thanked them and left the check.

"Can I ask you something, Jack?"

Jack picked up the check and took out his wallet. "Sure, what?"

"Do you ever think about staying in Seaport?"

He stilled, everything inside screaming for him to say yes, to tell her he wanted more than anything to stay in Seaport now that she would be there. "I can't, Ava."

Her smile faltered as she nodded.

"I've wanted to be a firefighter my whole life, to follow in my father's footsteps. It's all I've ever wanted to be, really, except for a brief moment in the sixth grade when I wanted to be an astronaut." Just one more reason he couldn't offer her more than friendship. He smiled, praying she'd understand. "Seaport only has a volunteer fire department. If I want a career as a firefighter, I have to stay in New York City or move elsewhere, and I don't want to go too far away from my mother."

"Sure, I get that." She shrugged it off as if it weren't all that important. "I was just wondering."

"What about you? Have you ever thought of moving to the city?" She hadn't been in Seaport that long, hadn't grown up there. He held his breath waiting for her answer, but she was already shaking her head.

"It's not the life I want for Missy, growing up amid so many strangers. More than anything, I want to give her a stable life surrounded by a small community of people who love her."

"You're right, of course." He was from Seaport, so he should know that better than anyone. "She'll be very happy there. It's a good place to grow up."

His heart ached, but he couldn't think of anything else to say, so he simply stood to pay the bill. For just a moment, the thought of commuting to the city for work flashed into his head, and he dismissed it just as quickly.

Ava smiled. "Thank you. I didn't even realize how hungry I was, but that was delicious, and I do feel better now, more awake and ready to do this drive. I don't like being away from Missy this long."

She always made it seem like the most natural thing in the world to put Missy first no matter what decisions she was making. To some men, that might seem off-putting. Not to Jack. In his mind, children should always come first. It was a selfless, admirable quality. The kind of quality he'd look for in a wife—if he ever planned on marrying again.

As Jack laid a hand on the small of Ava's back and

guided her through the door the hostess held open, he was struck by the realization of how petite and delicate she really was. He nodded to the hostess. "Thank you."

"Sure. Come again."

As soon as the door closed behind them, he scanned the lot looking for Pat and found him parked in a spot not far from the door, then he continued to let his gaze play over the lot, the buildings facing the lot, the parked cars. He'd do well to remember, while one of Ava's attackers had been caught, the other had gotten away and could be anywhere.

"Come on." Since he couldn't surround Ava with a bulletproof shield, he settled for gripping her hand and jogging across the lot. A full-out run would draw too much attention, but the quicker they made it to the vehicle, the safer they'd be. "Hurry."

She seemed to understand his sense of urgency and kept her head down as she rushed to the dark gray sedan, a great inconspicuous car that would hopefully be in one piece when they returned it to Pat.

Pat held out a hand, and Jack shook it. "Thanks, man, I owe you one."

"You owe me more than one, my man." He winked at Ava. "There's a cooler on the back seat filled with drinks and a bunch of sandwiches so you don't have to get out of the car any more than necessary."

"You're the best, Pat." Jack hugged him and patted his back. "Thanks. Now, get out of here."

The last thing he wanted was for anyone to go after Pat for helping them.

Pat hugged Ava and wished her well, then strolled across the lot toward the train station, hands stuffed in his pockets as if out for a casual walk.

Ava slid quickly into the passenger seat and looked after him. "He's a good friend."

"He is, has been since we were kids." And Jack could only pray he wouldn't have any trouble because he'd helped them. He was beginning to understand some of Ava's reluctance to involve the people she'd come to care about in her life. Since Pat had left the car running, Jack buckled his seat belt, checked behind him and shifted into Reverse.

Ava chewed on her lower lip. "I wish we weren't getting started so late."

So did Jack, but there was no sense worrying over something they couldn't change. "Don't worry about it. We should hit less traffic now and still be able to make it to the bank early enough tomorrow morning that we can follow up on any leads we might find."

As long as Ava's attacker didn't find them again.

TEN

Ava drummed her fingers against the steering wheel. What had she been thinking, letting Jack go into the bank alone? How had she allowed him to talk her into waiting in the car? And what was taking him so long? "Come on, come on, come on."

Oh, right, he'd convinced her someone going in alone wouldn't draw as much attention as both of them going in together, especially if anyone who could identify her was watching. And he was probably right. But what if he was wrong? What if her stalker knew to watch the bank? "Get a grip, Ava. If he knew to look at the bank, he wouldn't have needed to come after you."

She turned up the air conditioner and aimed the vent at her face, needing the cool air. Lifting her hair off her neck, she kept a firm gaze on the front door, until her eyes started to blur. She closed them for an instant, took a deep breath and opened them again.

Jack strolled out of the bank, hands tucked into his pockets, a small bag—

Her heart stuttered.

A small bag was casually slung over his shoulder. He'd found something.

She let her hair fall back into place and sat up straighter as he looked both ways and ran across the narrow side street, then opened the door, tossed the bag with the bank's logo onto the back seat and hopped in.

"You found something?"

"Yeah." He checked the side-view mirror, looked around them, over his shoulder, then back at her. "But let's get out of here before we go through it all."

He didn't have to tell her twice. As much as she wanted to know what was in that bag, goose bumps raised the hair on her arms. It was time to move. She shifted into gear, glanced behind her and pulled out onto the one-way street. The thought of getting to the house they'd rented and opening the bag only to find nothing of interest practically brought tears to her eyes. "Did you look inside?"

"I opened it enough to see there are papers inside." He turned to look at her, studied her face while she drove. "And an envelope addressed to someone named Angelina. I assume that's your real name."

Everything in her stilled, froze in that moment. Her real name. The name of the woman she'd been before all of this. The name her attacker had so harshly whispered against her ear. The woman who'd ceased to exist the moment she went on the run.

A letter to her could only mean one thing: Liam had known he might not make it. Maybe he'd simply left her a goodbye or an apology. Or maybe it was evidence that could put an end to this nightmare. No matter what was in that envelope, the only thing she was certain of was that Liam had left it to her.

"Ava…" Jack reached out, caught a tear she hadn't

felt rolling down her cheek with his thumb. "Why don't you pull over, take a minute to collect yourself? I can drive if you want."

"The house is only a few minutes away, I can wait until we get there." She shook her head and wiped the rest of her tears with the back of her wrist. At least then she'd be alone and wouldn't draw any attention to them if she lost the battle for control of her emotions. She was barely holding on by a thread as it was.

"How's Missy?"

Jarred by the change of subject, she glanced over at Jack. "How did you know I talked to her?"

"Oh, please." He laughed. "I figure I was barely across the street before you were on the phone."

She smiled through the tears, grateful he understood her need to talk about anything other than the contents of that bag. "She's doing okay, but Serena said she had a rough night. Bad dreams."

Jack looked out the window, checked the side mirror. "Can't blame her, really, but I have a feeling it'll all be over soon, and then both of you can begin to heal and move on."

Was that true? Could she heal after all this time? Could she learn to trust someone so completely she'd be able to give her heart to him again? She didn't know. But for the first time, she began to wonder if doing the right thing, finding out who'd killed Liam and bringing him to justice, would allow her the closure she'd need to begin a new life.

In silence, they drove the remaining ten miles to the small lakeside cottage Pat had arranged for them,

Ava lost in thoughts of the past, Missy, and the slightest blossom of hope for a future.

Jack seemed lost in thought as well, and she wondered what he was thinking about, but she didn't ask. Maybe she wasn't ready for the answer.

She pulled into the narrow driveway, shifted into Reverse and kept her foot on the brake as Jack had instructed, while he got out and walked the perimeter of the house.

When he disappeared around the far side, she held her breath until he returned and grabbed the bag from the back seat, opened her door and ushered her inside as quickly as possible. He set the bag on the kitchen table, then took the car key from her. "Why don't you go ahead and take a look. I'm going to go move the car."

Confused, she frowned. "Move it where?"

"I just want to turn it around so it's facing the street if we have to move quickly."

She nodded, knowing he could have told her to reverse into the driveway, grateful he'd given her the chance to be alone with Liam for a few moments. She didn't sit, couldn't with her nerves strung so tight. Instead, she pulled the bag closer to her, ran shaky fingers over the zipper, prayed for the answers she needed, the courage to do what had to be done with whatever information she found, and the strength to get through the next few minutes. Tears dripped onto the bag as she unzipped it.

A business-sized envelope sat on top, her name scrawled across the front in Liam's sloppy cursive. A laugh bubbled out with a sob. His penmanship had always been something she'd teased him about. He'd leave her a list for the market, and she'd have to decipher what exactly he wanted. Half the time she got it wrong.

"Oh, Liam…" Her hands trembled as she opened the envelope and pulled out a folded piece of paper. When her legs started to shake, she pulled out a chair, sat and carefully unfolded the letter.

My dearest Angelina,
If you are reading this, it means things didn't go as planned. Know first how sorry I am. Sorry to have involved you in this. Sorry I had to leave you. You are the love of my life, and leaving you would be my biggest regret. Well… I guess my second biggest regret. Putting you in danger would be first. And have no doubt, you are in danger and will be until you can expose the corruption I've uncovered or disappear.

She sniffed and wiped her tears so she could see the words—words he'd obviously taken the time to pen carefully so there'd be no mistaking what he wanted to say.

My plan is to go to the police, give them copies of some of what I've uncovered and see if they can be trusted. If anything happens to me, they can't be. You will find documents here, detailing the arson spree that is plaguing our neighborhood, along with proof that Alan Hayes, a fellow firefighter and the chief's son, is responsible. I've not gone to the local police before now because Chief Hayes is close to many of the higher-ups in the department. I have no choice but to try, though I don't trust anyone at this point.

Except you. If you've found this bag, I can only assume you took the flight bag, got out and found the key to my safe deposit box. I pray this letter finds you safe and unharmed. Whatever you choose to do with this information is up to you. If you do decide to turn it over to the authorities, do not go to the local police. If you want to burn it all or just leave it in the box indefinitely, I will understand. I trust you with everything in me and have no doubt you will make the right choice, whatever that might be.

Please know, you are the love of my life, and I am so very sorry if this cost us being together, but I had to do what I felt was right. I wrestled with the decision when I realized who was involved, but in the end, there were fatalities in some of the fires he set, and I couldn't let anyone else die. I couldn't live with that. I hope you understand.

I will always love you, and I pray you find happiness.

All my love,

Liam

Ava read the letter through twice more. Her hands shook wildly as she folded the letter and returned it to the envelope, then clutched it to her chest, crying softly for what had been taken from her. Liam had trusted her, trusted her to find the information he'd left, trusted her to do the right thing, and she felt like she'd failed him.

She'd run instead of following through on something that was important enough for him to give his life for.

A hand settled on her shoulder, and she looked up into Jack's eyes. He'd stood by her, helped her, protected her and Missy. He deserved to know.

Without a word, she handed him the letter. He read it quickly, then tucked it back into the envelope and set it on the table. With one hand on the table, and one on the back of the chair, he crouched in front of her, looked her straight in the eye. "He didn't know about Missy, Ava. If he had known, he'd have told you to forget everything and run."

"How can you know that?" She sobbed and lowered her gaze.

He lifted her chin, caught her gaze. "Because it's what I would have wanted. Liam trusted you completely, knew you'd make the right choice, and you did."

She nodded. He was right. Had Liam known about Missy, he'd have expected Ava to put her first. And if he didn't, he wouldn't have been the man she knew he was. "Thank you for that."

He smiled, stood and laid a hand on hers. "Anytime. Now, why don't we see what evidence he left, figure out what to do with it and get home to Mischief."

She sucked in a deep breath and nodded. "Sounds like a plan."

They spent the next hour going through the paperwork Liam had left. He'd kept a journal from the time he first started to suspect someone in the department was covering up fires that had been deliberately set, detailed dates and times and reports that had disappeared. It was clear more than one person was involved in the cover-up, but it had taken him months to figure out any of them. There were photos as well, pictures he must have taken just before he was killed. One of them showed a man Ava didn't recognize but assumed was Alan Hayes carrying a jug into a building, the same man walking away with flames starting to lick at the windows.

Jack set up the laptop he'd brought with them and inserted the flash drive they'd also found in the bag. They scrolled through document after document, investigative reports that proved arson, that, according to Liam's journal, had later disappeared. Several arrest reports were also included. "Assault, assault and battery and hmm… Here's one for trespassing. Apparently, Alan Hayes was arrested for trespassing on one of the properties that later burned down."

Ava started packing everything back into the bag. "If we turn all of the evidence over to your friend, Gabe, can he figure out who to contact?"

Jack nodded absently as he typed something on the computer.

"Fine, that's what we'll do." She returned everything except the letter to the bag, then put the letter into her purse, careful not to crumple it. "Let's get some sleep and we can head back to Long Island."

"Well, well, well…" Jack let out a low whistle and turned the laptop to face her. "Will ya look at that."

"What?"

"Seems our Mr. Hayes has political ambitions to go along with that hot temper." He pointed to an article he had up on the screen. It seemed Alan Hayes, who was definitely the man in the photos, was running for mayor.

"Coming after you now makes a whole lot more sense knowing there's an election soon."

"Yeah, but won't his arrests keep him from being elected?" Who would want to elect a criminal mayor?

"The arrests themselves? Probably not, since there are no convictions." He pulled the computer back and typed some more, muttering as he tried to find whatever he was looking for. "Also, apparently, the arrest records are gone. At least from what I can tell. I guess the arson reports aren't the only documents to go missing. And I can see now why Liam didn't trust the police."

"I don't understand. Why would someone who's now running for mayor have burned down a bunch of buildings, some of which had people inside? It doesn't make sense."

Jack held out a notebook he took from the bag. "It does if he was laundering money, running illegal gambling rings, storing and selling weapons, along with numerous other scams, and trying to rid himself of the competition. Also, there's been cases before of firemen starting fires so they could be the hero. That would certainly look good for a man with political aspirations."

"Except he never saved anyone." She couldn't imagine what had gone through Liam's mind when he'd figured out what was going on. He had worked with this man, trusted him to have his back. She started to scan the pages. "Liam figured all this out?"

"Apparently, he was watching him for a few months at least." Jack tapped the open notebook.

"Why didn't he go to the FBI or something?" Anger had begun to creep in, nudging aside some of the renewed grief.

"I only skimmed through these books, but I don't think he knew who was involved at first. He was studying the buildings that were burned. At some point he figured out what they were being used for. Then, later, he learned who was involved, that it was a fellow firefighter, a man he'd have trusted with his life."

She sighed and sat back. All she wanted to do was go home, turn all of this over to a police officer Jack trusted and move on. And then it hit her like a fist to the gut, stole her breath. She could move on. If Gabe contacted someone who could arrest Alan Hayes, and he was convicted of Liam's murder and the arsons, she'd be free to stay in Seaport, build a life with Missy… Her gaze shot to Jack.

Was there a chance the two of them could get to know each other better? Maybe see if there could ever be something more than friendship between them? Maybe. Except for one thing, Jack wasn't staying in Seaport. He couldn't. And she'd never ask him to give up what he loved, an honor to his father, for any reason. Besides, none of that would alter the pain of losing the child he'd loved. Nor would it change his feelings about getting involved with another woman with a child.

She wasn't quite ready to deal with the disappointment that thought brought. "If we sleep for a few hours, do you think we can start back later today?"

Jack stuffed the rest of what he'd been looking through back into the bag along with the laptop, then hitched it onto his shoulder. "We're getting out of here now. If we get tired, we can pull over at a rest stop and sleep along the way."

His sudden sense of urgency startled her. "What's wrong?"

"I don't know…" He looked out the window over the sink into the small yard that bordered a woods and swamp. "Get down."

Jack shoved Ava to the floor and leaned over her as the back window imploded and a flaming projectile flew overhead, landed in the living room and exploded. Her assailant must have followed them somehow, and they'd led him straight to everything he needed to get away with all he'd done. No way would Jack let that happen.

Heat scorched his back. He hooked Ava beneath the arm and propelled her toward the back door. "Go."

Keeping low, hands over her head, she ran in the direction he'd indicated.

He grabbed her purse from the table. Even though he had all the evidence in the bag on his shoulder, Liam's letter was in her purse, and that was irreplaceable.

A second crash came from the front of the house, no doubt another Molotov cocktail thrown through the front window, followed by a second explosion. Fueled by the accelerant, flames raced through the kitchen and living room, voraciously consuming everything in their path.

"Wait." Ava whirled back. "I can't leave—"

He handed her the purse, and her gaze caught and held his.

No time to spare. Hopefully, they'd have a minute or two before the guy could get back around and over the gate from the front of the house. But not much longer than that. "Head straight for the woods as fast as you can. Don't look back."

"But won't he expect that this time?"

"Probably, but there's no choice." He whipped the door open. "Now go!"

She ran across the small yard and into the woods with him on her heels, trying his best to cover her. No way would the man leave without making sure she was dead this time, especially if he managed to get his hands on the bag.

A gunshot sounded way too close. Pain burst through his left arm, and he stumbled.

A second shot, and Ava went down, no more than a foot from the woods. She scrambled for cover, dove into the swampy brush and rolled.

"Ava." Jack tumbled in after her. Keeping his head down, he crawled to her. "Are you hurt?"

"My leg." She twisted around to get a better look at her calf. A small hole bled through her jeans.

The gunman would be on them in seconds. They had to move. "Can you walk?"

She gritted her teeth and struggled to her knees. "I'll crawl if I have to."

"Go, get deeper into the woods. Try to stay low and just find a place to hide." He didn't dare think about the consequences, the risk of infection from sending her into a swamp with a bullet wound in her leg. There was no other choice. He backed away as she started forward, then she looked over her shoulder.

"Wait. Where are you going?"

He put a finger against his lips and waved for her to go, then he crouched and backed against a huge gnarled tree trunk. The gunman was too close, and they were both injured. While he could run with his arm, she'd never outrun him with the bullet wound in her leg. Their only hope was if Jack could get behind him and catch him by surprise, then wrestle the gun from him.

Tears shimmered in her eyes as she stared at him another moment, then she turned away and crawled deeper into the reeds.

Footsteps pounded against the ground, the gunman coming fast across the yard. Too fast.

Ava moved a few more feet into the woods, then stopped and turned, crouching low, using the weeds and brush as camouflage. What was she doing? She had to move.

He tried to gesture for her to go, but she wasn't watching him. Instead, she kept her gaze riveted on the man barreling toward them.

Jack dropped his head back against the tree and sucked in a deep breath, waited… He'd only have one chance. He set the bag aside.

As the man reached the tree line, Ava threw something overhand. Something heavy that splashed into the murky pond several yards away.

The gunman paused, looked around, then plunged into the swamp in the direction of the splash. But he'd stood still long enough for Jack to be sure it was Alan Hayes. So he'd come himself instead of sending a hired gun or whatever cohorts he'd sent after her in New York. Probably couldn't resist the thought of burning Ava out, or he wanted to make sure the job got done right this time.

With a prayer for help, Jack lunged after him, took

him mid-body from behind, plowing his shoulder into the man's kidney and tackling him to the ground. He scrambled to keep hold of him in the slippery muck.

Hayes rolled over, hooked an arm around Jack's neck.

Jack grabbed his arm, tried to turn into him, to loosen the hold, but only managed to land a weak elbow to his sternum.

Hayes's grip loosened just enough for Jack to squirm free and slam his head into Hayes's face. Where was the gun? Hayes was fighting with both hands, which meant he'd either tucked it away, which didn't make sense, or he'd lost it. Hayes staggered to his knees.

Jack landed a solid kick to his ribs.

With a grunt, Hayes grabbed Jack around the ankle and yanked his foot out from under him, dropping him onto his back. On his knees, sucking in deep gulps of air, Hayes straddled him, fisted his hand and swung. He would have broken Jack's nose if he didn't turn his head away at the last minute. The punch landed against the side of his head instead.

Ears ringing, Jack bucked and threw Hayes off him. He got one knee underneath himself and tried to stand. Mud sucked at him, pulling his foot deeper, refusing to release his knee.

Hayes was on his hands and knees, feeling around in the mud, and he came up with the gun in his hand, aimed it at Jack.

Jack relaxed for an instant, just long enough to gain some wiggle room, then pulled his foot free, feinted right, then tucked and rolled left. He came up fast, grabbed hold of Hayes's gun hand and twisted, then kicked him in the stomach.

Hayes doubled over but held tight to the weapon.

Ava appeared out of nowhere, hooked an arm around Hayes's neck and gripped her other arm to tighten the hold.

Hayes clawed at her arms, swung blindly behind him, trying desperately to free himself, landing more than one blow, but Ava held tight. Finally, his eyes rolled up, and his grip on the gun loosened.

Jack grabbed it from him as Ava released him, and he fell on his side into the mud.

"Are you hurt?" he yelled to Ava even as he crawled through the muck to get to Hayes, feel for a pulse.

"Is he…" Ava's voice trembled.

"He's alive." Leaving him where he was and keeping the gun in his hand, even though it was so caked with mud Jack doubted it would work, he scrambled toward Ava. Sirens wailed in the distance, no doubt thanks to the explosion and fire. He was going to have to ask Ava to get back to the house and find help so he could stay with Hayes and make sure he didn't escape this time. But for this one moment…

Ignoring the filth covering his hand, and pretty much every other part of him and Ava, he knelt facing her, slid her mud-caked hair behind her ear and cupped her cheek. "Are you okay?"

She gripped his hand and nodded, tears leaving tracks through the dirt on her face, and she smiled at him.

His stomach dropped, free-falling as if he'd been knocked off a cliff, and he pressed his forehead against hers. All the pain, all the heartache, all the fear she'd suffered were over. Ava and Missy would be free now, free to settle down, free to live. Free to love, if only she could find a way to let go of the past and open her heart. "It's over, Ava. You're safe now. Missy is safe."

ELEVEN

As the sun began its descent into the bay amid an ocean of oranges and yellows, Ava lifted Missy into her arms and hugged her tight. In that instant, the emotions crept up on her, as they sometimes did, and she couldn't let go. Even now, a week after Hayes, his father, and a number of coconspirators were arrested, it was hard to believe her ordeal was really over. She couldn't know exactly where her life was going to take her, but she did know she was going to stay in Seaport, to give Missy a home where she could grow up feeling safe and secure among friends. "Come on, you, time to get going."

"Mama," she whined.

"Here…" Ava sat on a nearby bench, just for a minute to rest her leg and watch the sun set. Her leg still ached from the bullet wound, which sometimes made it difficult to chase after Missy, but she was recovering well. "You can play on my phone."

Missy settled against her and rubbed her eyes, then took the cell phone with a kids' game up and grinned as she started playing.

"Just don't push any other buttons." *Because I don't know how to fix it if you mess it up.*

Ava was always amazed that Missy could just pick up the phone and play games with no hesitation. Seemed kids were gifted with technological skills Ava hadn't been blessed with. But, at the moment, she was just grateful for a moment of quiet, for the sense of peace that washed over her with Missy safe and close.

As happy as she was to be at the beach having a picnic with the people who'd become so close to her, meant so much to her, stood by her when she'd needed help the most, she couldn't help the dull ache in her heart that had become her constant companion throughout the day, her last day with Jack.

The past week had flown by, faster than she ever would have dreamt possible. And Jack had barely left her side. She'd already known he was a good man and that there was something between them almost from the first time they'd met, but spending this past week together, getting to know each other better after all they'd been through, had led her to the true depths of her feelings for him. But he was set to go back to New York City the next day. Now that his sister and her kids had moved in with their mother, he had to return to his job, his apartment, his life. And she and Missy would stay in Seaport to begin their lives without him.

"Mind if I sit?" Miss Jenny pointed to the bench beside Ava. The two had become very close since Ava had returned from Florida, and Ava hoped that relationship would continue even after Jack left.

"Of course not, Miss Jenny."

"How are you feeling?"

"Better, thank you. My leg hardly hurts at all anymore unless I've been on it all day."

"Mm-hmm. I'm glad to hear that." The sun was a

giant ball of orange, casting a beautiful glow across the surface of the gently lapping water. Miss Jenny stared out over the bay with a hint of sadness touching her eyes. "This has always been my favorite time of day at the beach."

"Mine too."

"I remember I used to sit out here with my husband and watch the sunset, always such a peaceful time." She frowned. "Funny, isn't it? That some memories should be so clear, as if they happened only yesterday, and others…ah well…" She waved a hand dismissively. "You seem happier. Anyway, that's how you seem to me since you returned from Florida…maybe happier isn't the right word, but more content, more at peace."

"Missy is my whole world, and I missed her terribly. I'm just happy to be home with her now."

"Believe me, I understand how that is. I suppose you know how rampant gossip runs in a town this size."

Used to the rapid changes in subject, Ava switched gears easily. "No kidding. Working in a shop in town, I sometimes know things before the people involved do."

"I suppose you would." Miss Jenny stood and picked up a piece of beach glass worn smooth by time from amid the seashells, seaweed and rocks scattered along the waterline where the tide had receded. She brushed the sand off and returned to her seat at Ava's side. "So, I'm sure you'll understand I've heard rumors about what brought you out here—some accurate, others probably not so much."

Ava nodded, her lips closed tight over her clenched teeth. Once the story had broken about Alan Hayes's arrest, even the national news outlets had picked it up, so now half of Seaport knew about her buried secrets.

The fact the story had made the front page of every paper around probably didn't help.

"Now, this is none of my business, dear, and feel free to tell an old lady to butt out, but I've been watching my Jacky lately, and I watched him while he was talking to you on the phone earlier." She shook her head. "I haven't seen him that happy in quite a while."

Miss Jenny paused, toed her sandals off and dug her feet into the warm sand. Looking out over the water, she sighed. "I've lived my whole life on this island. Anyway... What was I saying? Oh, right. I don't know how much you and Jack have talked, or how much you know about me, but I lost my husband, a firefighter just like your Liam, when my kids were very young."

Ava gasped before she could cover her surprise that Miss Jenny was sharing this with her. In the time since she'd met Miss Jenny, the other woman had never once talked about her past.

"I've lived a very rewarding life. My children have always been everything, and I wouldn't change that for the world, but it can be a lonely road. My Jeremy, he was a compassionate man, and he would have understood if I'd met someone else, but I wouldn't allow myself the opportunity to move on." She turned to face Ava, a tear rolling down her cheek. "Don't get me wrong, I have not a single regret, but..."

Ava resisted the urge to wrap her arms around the fragile woman, wanting to give her the opportunity to say her piece.

She frowned and shook her head. "I get sidetracked so easily now. Anyway, I just wanted to say losing Jeremy was the hardest thing I've ever done, the most painful experience I've ever lived through. But, with

God's help, I did make it through. I can tell you've found peace, dear. But don't be afraid to find happiness now."

Ava didn't say anything, couldn't, so she simply nodded.

"Anyway, I should get back to helping Serena clean up. Forgive me for intruding, dear. I just figured I'd better say my piece while I was thinking of it." Her eyes clouded over, and she quickly lowered her gaze to her hands intertwined in front of her. "Things tend to slip my mind so quickly these days."

She paused, seeming lost in thought, then grinned, and for just a moment, Ava could see her son in the mischievous smile. "Of course, some of my motives for talking to you are purely selfish. I've long hoped Jack would find the right woman and come home to Seaport to stay."

Ava's heart stuttered, and she covered the momentary leap of hope with a nervous laugh. Jack had never given any indication he was going to return to Seaport to live. He seemed to enjoy his life in the city, and Ava didn't dare hope she would be enough to change that. Especially since she had a little girl, a little girl she'd seen Jack's affection for. No way was he going to get involved with her and risk having his heart shattered again. Not that she blamed him.

When she'd been in that swamp, fully focused on saving Jack, on escaping Hayes and returning to the little girl she loved more than anything else, she'd come to realize it was worth risking your heart for the chance to love someone so completely. Unfortunately, Jack hadn't come to that same conclusion, or he wouldn't be leaving, wouldn't have spent the past day at his mother's packing up his things.

Miss Jenny patted her hand and ruffled Missy's curls, then stood and stepped back into her sandals. "You make sure to be on time for the bonfire."

"I will." Ava nodded. "And, Miss Jenny, thank you."

She smiled, then turned and walked away.

Ava watched the sun's slow dip into the bay, fascinated, as always, by the swirl of colors reflected there. Miss Jenny's words played over in her mind. Did she really want to spend the rest of her life alone but for Missy? Missy was her whole world, but the thought of having someone to share her life with, share her children with, to grow old with, had started to take hold now that she was finally free from her past.

But Jack was leaving.

"She's really playing." Jack leaned over the back of the bench to see the screen Missy was engrossed in.

She laughed at his surprise. "She can do anything on this thing. She plays games, takes pictures...and thankfully calls 911 in an emergency."

"Big Earl." Missy smiled up at her.

She ruffled Missy's curls. "Yup. Every time we call 911, Big Earl comes."

"And Fireman Jack," she added.

"That's right, Fireman Jack came last time." But he wouldn't anymore. She held back tears. "But we only call in an emergency, right?"

"Uh-huh." But her attention had already returned to her game.

"That phone case is great."

She forced a smile. "Hard to believe they make a case that's even Missy-proof."

He frowned. "Hopefully, there will be no more need for nine-one-one calls."

A very unladylike snort blurted out before Ava could contain it. "Somehow I doubt that."

Jack laughed, and Missy reached for his hand.

He sat beside Ava, keeping Missy's hand in his.

"It's not that she doesn't listen. She actually listens really well most of the time, other than an occasional, typical-three-year-old tantrum—usually when she's overtired. But, even though she's kind of mature for her age, she doesn't always know her limitations." Great, now she was rambling because she had no idea what to say to him. It's not like he was moving to another country or anything, and he could always hop on the Long Island Rail Road and come visit on his days off, but it wouldn't be the same. She wanted so badly for him to stay, but his life was elsewhere, and his heart was still broken.

Ava looked great, her cheeks pink with sunburn from playing with Mischief on the beach all day. Waning sunlight reflected off her golden curls as the wind whipped strands of hair across her face. It was good to see her up and around again. Thankfully, he still held Missy's hand in his, or he might not have resisted the urge to reach out and tuck the loose strands behind her ear.

If he were to be honest with himself, which he always tried to be, he'd have to say he'd miss this. A lot. As much as he loved the city, there was nothing like a barbecue on the beach at sunset with family and friends.

A few children still laughed and ran around the playground and along the beach. Seagulls screamed and dove, snatching whatever they could find. He inhaled deeply, filling his lungs with the salty scent of the sea that had been part of his earliest childhood memories.

She watched him, tears shimmering in her eyes, and he dared to hope they were for him, that she wanted him to stay. "Are you ready for the bonfire?"

"Just about." His voice cracked, and he cleared his throat.

Ava smiled, and he was lost. Every argument he'd used to talk himself out of getting closer to her fled his mind. When he'd first met her, he'd been attracted to her, but she'd seemed so vulnerable, he'd wanted to take care of her. As time went on and he got to know her better, he realized that couldn't be further from the truth, and he'd come to respect her, admire her, love her. He could admit it now, even if it had taken a while. But when he'd seen her in that swamp, injured, filthy, terrified, holding a killer in a choke hold to save his life, he'd gone over an edge there was no coming back from. She could have run, could have fled deeper into the swamp or hidden or just froze, but she didn't. Instead, she'd stood up to her attacker, faced her fears head-on, found the courage to stand not only for herself and for Liam, but for him too.

"You ready?"

He looked up to find Ava in front of him, Mischief in her arms. "Huh?"

Mischief bounced up and down and yanked her hand away to clap. "S'mores!"

Ava held a hand out to him. "Need a hand?"

"Uh…" What had they been talking about? He shook his head in an effort to bring himself back to reality. *Oh, right. The bonfire.* "Sure."

She frowned and tilted her head. "Everything okay?"

"Yes, uh, no, I mean…" He took her hand but remained where he was. "Ava, could you please sit with me for another moment?"

She glanced at Missy. "I can try, but there's no guarantee."

He laughed, and suddenly all of his inhibitions were swept away with the evening breeze. "It'll just take a minute, I promise."

Missy scrunched up her face. "S'mores."

"Yup. But first, I have something for you." He waited for Ava to sit, to settle Missy on her lap.

"Surprise?" Mischief grinned.

"Yes, but Mama first, okay?"

She nodded eagerly, bouncing her curls, so much like her mother's, into her face.

"Thank you. For everything." Ava held his gaze, and a blush crept up her cheeks, coloring them even redder than the sun had. "This was fun. I'm really glad we came."

"Me too." A small rush of pleasure shot through him, and he finally gave in and tucked the hair that had blown across her face behind her ear, then took her hand in his. "If someone had told me a few weeks ago I'd decide to stay in Seaport when my leave of absence was over, I'd have argued there was no way. And then I met you. And Mischief. And the thought of going back to the city leaves me feeling incomplete, like there's a hole in my center that nothing can fill."

Ava's fingers fluttered to her mouth, and one tear tipped over. "But I thought…"

"I know. I thought too, but I guess we were both wrong." He laughed. It had taken the thought of losing her to make him realize how much she meant to him, to realize being with her was worth the risk of losing her. And Missy, if Ava decided to walk away. But for now...

"I love you, Ava, with everything in me. You and Missy both. I've decided to stay in Seaport, if you want that."

"I do, Jack, so much, and I love you too, and I want more than anything for you to be happy. I don't want to be the cause of you giving up what you love."

"I won't be giving it up." He'd thought a lot about it, and Ava was right. He didn't want to see Missy grow up in the city. He wanted her to grow up here, where he had, among family and friends. "I can continue with Seaport Fire and Rescue on a volunteer basis, but they have no paid firefighters. Neither do any of the surrounding towns. Hopefully, someday, that will change, but until it does, I'm going to commute.

"I want to buy a nice little house with a big yard and a garden and a white picket fence, right here in Seaport, and I want you and Missy to share it with me."

Her tears flowed freely, as Jack slid to one knee and held out the ring he'd spent yesterday shopping for when he should have been packing. "Ava, will you marry me?"

"Yes," she sobbed. "I will. I love you, Jack, with all of my heart."

He slid the ring onto her finger, kissed her, then took Missy's hand in his. "Honey, I don't know if you understand what it means to get engaged."

She looked at her mother, then returned her gaze to his and shook her head.

"Well, it's like a promise to get married and to care for one another forever."

"Are you gonna care for Mama?"

"I am, yes, and I'm going to care for you too." He held out a delicate gold bracelet. "Would you like that?"

"You mean like a daddy, like Kiara has Big Earl?"

"Yes, just like that."

"Yes!"

He clasped the bracelet onto her wrist, and she launched herself from Ava's lap to throw her arms around his neck. He hugged her tight, held a hand out for Ava's and pulled her into his embrace as well. And in that moment, his life was perfect. Well, almost…

"I like my surprise." Missy studied the bracelet. "Shiny."

"Yes, it is shiny, but that's only part of your surprise."

"More?"

"Yup, come with me." He took one of Missy's hands, and Ava took the other. Together, the three of them crossed the beach to a patch of grass where a small gated enclosure had been set up beneath the streetlights.

The instant she realized what was corralled in the enclosure, Mischief squealed, shrugged out of their grips and ran forward. "Puppies!"

Jack looked at Ava and grinned. "There's one more thing I wanted to talk to you about."

Ava laughed, and in that moment, his life was perfect.

* * * * *

If you enjoyed Shielding the Tiny Target,
*pick up this other thrilling story
from Deena Alexander:*

Crime Scene Connection

*Available now from Love Inspired Suspense!
Find more great reads at
www.LoveInspired.com*

Dear Reader,

Thank you so much for sharing Jack and Ava's story! I love flawed characters, whose internal conflicts are as unique and challenging as the danger they find themselves in.

One of the things both Jack and Ava struggle with is the ability to trust. They've both been hurt in the past and are having a difficult time learning to trust again. I think all of us go through trials in our lives that make it difficult to open up and trust one another, but as long as we continue to trust in God, I believe we can learn to trust others again.

I hope you've enjoyed sharing Jack and Ava's journey as much as I enjoyed creating it. If you'd like to keep up with me, you can find me on Facebook at Facebook.com/DeenaAlexanderAuthor, and on Twitter at Twitter.com/DeenaAlexanderA.

Deena Alexander

COMING NEXT MONTH FROM
Love Inspired Suspense

TRACKING A KILLER
Rocky Mountain K-9 Unit • by Elizabeth Goddard
The last thing K-9 officer Harlow Zane expected when she and cadaver dog Nell join an investigation is to draw the killer's obsessive attention. But FBI special agent Wes Grey notices she matches the victim profile, and when another look-alike goes missing, they must work together to catch the criminal...before Harlow's the next to disappear.

HIDING IN PLAIN SIGHT
by Laura Scott
Fleeing to her uncle's home is Shauna McKay's only option after her mother's brutally murdered and the murderer's sights set on her. Local sheriff Liam Harland's convinced hiding Shauna in an Amish community will shield her—until an Amish woman who looks like Shauna is attacked. It's clear nobody in this peaceful community is safe...

FUGITIVE AMBUSH
Range River Bounty Hunters • by Jenna Night
While pursuing a dangerous bail jumper, bounty hunter Hayley Ryan barely escapes an attack by the fugitive. Teaming up with rival Jack Colter results in the discovery of another criminal—one who's been missing for years. Can their uneasy partnership—and lives—survive their search for not one but two notorious escaped felons?

ROCKY MOUNTAIN VENDETTA
by Jane M. Choate
With her husband's killer released from prison and dead set on revenge, former US marshal Brianna Thomas's fake identity's no longer enough to protect her and her little girl. Now snowbound in the Rockies with the only person she can trust, ex-marshal Gideon Stratham, she must survive a storm *and* the convict's vengeance.

TWIN MURDER MIX-UP
Deputies of Anderson County • by Sami A. Abrams
After capturing a murder on camera, photographer Amy Baker becomes the next target—and her identical twin is killed instead. Now on the run with her sister's newborn, Amy turns to Detective Keith Young, her childhood crush. But when they discover Keith is the baby's father, can he regain Amy's trust...before the killer strikes again?

ESCAPE ROUTE
by Tanya Stowe
While flying above the Texas border, helicopter pilot Tara Jean "TJ" Baskins witnesses a ruthless murder. Now a deadly gang wants her out of the way. Border patrol officer Trace Leyton—her old friend and the man who once betrayed her—is determined to catch the ring's leader...until the search leads to Trace's family.

LOOK FOR THESE AND OTHER LOVE INSPIRED BOOKS WHEREVER BOOKS ARE SOLD, INCLUDING MOST BOOKSTORES, SUPERMARKETS, DISCOUNT STORES AND DRUGSTORES.

LISCNM0722

Get 4 FREE REWARDS!

We'll send you 2 FREE Books plus 2 FREE Mystery Gifts.

FREE Value Over **$20**

Both the **Love Inspired®** and **Love Inspired® Suspense** series feature compelling novels filled with inspirational romance, faith, forgiveness, and hope.

YES! Please send me 2 FREE novels from the Love Inspired or Love Inspired Suspense series and my 2 FREE gifts (gifts are worth about $10 retail). After receiving them, if I don't wish to receive any more books, I can return the shipping statement marked "cancel." If I don't cancel, I will receive 6 brand-new Love Inspired Larger-Print books or Love Inspired Suspense Larger-Print books every month and be billed just $5.99 each in the U.S. or $6.24 each in Canada. That is a savings of at least 17% off the cover price. It's quite a bargain! Shipping and handling is just 50¢ per book in the U.S. and $1.25 per book in Canada.* I understand that accepting the 2 free books and gifts places me under no obligation to buy anything. I can always return a shipment and cancel at any time. The free books and gifts are mine to keep no matter what I decide.

Choose one: ☐ **Love Inspired**
Larger-Print
(122/322 IDN GNWC)

☐ **Love Inspired Suspense**
Larger-Print
(107/307 IDN GNWN)

Name (please print)

Address   Apt. #

City   State/Province   Zip/Postal Code

Email: Please check this box ☐ if you would like to receive newsletters and promotional emails from Harlequin Enterprises ULC and its affiliates. You can unsubscribe anytime.

Mail to the **Harlequin Reader Service:**
IN U.S.A.: P.O. Box 1341, Buffalo, NY 14240-8531
IN CANADA: P.O. Box 603, Fort Erie, Ontario L2A 5X3

Want to try 2 free books from another series! Call 1-800-873-8635 or visit www.ReaderService.com.

---

*Terms and prices subject to change without notice. Prices do not include sales taxes, which will be charged (if applicable) based on your state or country of residence. Canadian residents will be charged applicable taxes. Offer not valid in Quebec. This offer is limited to one order per household. Books received may not be as shown. Not valid for current subscribers to the Love Inspired or Love Inspired Suspense series. All orders subject to approval. Credit or debit balances in a customer's account(s) may be offset by any other outstanding balance owed by or to the customer. Please allow 4 to 6 weeks for delivery. Offer available while quantities last.

Your Privacy—Your information is being collected by Harlequin Enterprises ULC, operating as Harlequin Reader Service. For a complete summary of the information we collect, how we use this information and to whom it is disclosed, please visit our privacy notice located at corporate.harlequin.com/privacy-notice. From time to time we may also exchange your personal information with reputable third parties. If you wish to opt out of this sharing of your personal information, please visit readerservice.com/consumerschoice or call 1-800-873-8635. **Notice to California Residents**—Under California law, you have specific rights to control and access your data. For more information on these rights and how to exercise them, visit corporate.harlequin.com/california-privacy.

LIRLIS22

SPECIAL EXCERPT FROM

LOVE INSPIRED SUSPENSE

INSPIRATIONAL ROMANCE

Fleeing to her uncle's home is Shauna McKay's only option after her mother's brutally murdered and the murderer's sights set on her. Local sheriff Liam Harland's convinced hiding Shauna in an Amish community will shield her. But it's clear nobody in this peaceful community is safe…

Read on for a sneak preview of
Hiding in Plain Sight *by Laura Scott,*
available September 2022 from Love Inspired Suspense!

Someone was shooting at them!

Liam hit the gas and Shauna braced herself for the worst. Her body began to shake uncontrollably as the SUV sped up and jerked from side to side as Liam attempted to escape.

They were shooting at her this time. Not just attempting to run her off the road.

These people, whoever they were, wanted her *dead*.

Just like her mother.

Why? She couldn't seem to grasp why she'd suddenly become a target. It just didn't make any sense. Tears pricked her eyes, but she held them back.

After what seemed like eons but was likely only fifteen minutes, the vehicle slowed to a normal rate of speed.

"Are you okay?" Liam asked tersely.

She hesitantly lifted her head, scanning the area. "I— Yes. You?"

"Fine. Thankfully the shooter missed us. I wish I knew exactly where the gunfire came from." He sounded frustrated. "This is my fault. I knew you were in danger, but I didn't expect anyone to fire at us in broad daylight."

"At me." Her voice was soft but firm. "Not you, Liam. This is all about me."

He glanced sharply at her. "They could have easily shot me, too, Shauna. Thankfully, they missed, but that was too close. And you still don't know why these people have come after you?" He hesitated, then added, "Or why they killed your mother?"

"No." She shrugged helplessly. "I'm not lying. There is no reason I can come up with that would cause this sort of action. No one hated either of us this much."

"Revenge?" He divided his attention between her and the road. She didn't recognize the highway they were on, but then again, she didn't know much of anything about Green Lake.

Other than she'd brought danger to the quaint tourist town.

Don't miss
Hiding in Plain Sight *by Laura Scott,*
available September 2022 wherever
Love Inspired Suspense books and ebooks are sold.

LoveInspired.com

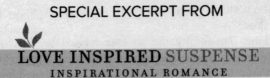
Busy's Amish Market still smelled the same, like fresh bread, strawberries, lemon furniture polish and clean cotton. Jackson Lapp hadn't thought much about Busy's during the past twelve years. It was easier to try to forget his former life instead of dwelling on the things he couldn't have anymore.

As he walked farther into the crowded and cluttered store, Jackson struggled to get his bearings. No, that wasn't exactly true. He was actually coming up with a number of reasons it would be best for everyone—most especially himself—if he simply walked right back out the door.

But every time he thought about the way the girl had been found, in the back room of a seedy hotel with needle marks in her arm, he felt sick to his stomach. Seeing the discarded *kapp* neatly folded in the tote under that cot had nearly taken his breath away. The girl, obviously still a teenager, had been Amish.

LISEXP426093

LOVE INSPIRED

Stories to uplift and inspire

Fall in love with Love Inspired—
inspirational and uplifting stories of faith
and hope. Find strength and comfort in
the bonds of friendship and community.
Revel in the warmth of possibility and the
promise of new beginnings.

Sign up for the Love Inspired newsletter
at **LoveInspired.com** to be the first
to find out about upcoming titles,
special promotions and exclusive content.

CONNECT WITH US AT:

 Facebook.com/LoveInspiredBooks

Twitter.com/LoveInspiredBks

It was only when he'd taken a closer look at one of the crime scene photographs that he'd felt a ray of hope. That *kapp* had been found in a signature tote from Busy's Amish Market.

Busy Troyer, the owner of the Amish market, had long since gone to the Lord. He wasn't even sure who ran the market now, but there was a very good chance whoever it was would be reluctant to help him. Not too many Amish wanted much to do with an *Englischer* cop from Cincinnati.

But he still had to try.

Glad that the woman behind the counter was busy helping customers, Jackson kept to the outside aisles of the store. Memories overwhelmed him. This store held some of the best moments in his life.

But the memories that mattered most were the ones that had to do with the pretty girl he'd met at the store. LizBeth Troyer.

They'd become fast friends when they were nine. They'd annoyed each other to no end when they were thirteen. And he'd fallen in love with LizBeth when he was sixteen.

He'd even tried to kiss her once in the very aisle he was standing in.

Looking at all the pots, pans and serving spoons, Jackson blinked. Why had he even wandered over in that direction?

"Can I help you?"

He started, then gaped as he found the owner of the sweet, then melodic voice. "LizBeth," he said before he could remind himself to keep quiet.

A haunted look appeared on her face. No doubt it was a match to his own expression. Ignoring the five or so people who'd just walked to the counter, she stepped toward him.

She was still perfect and beautiful and had a way of looking at him that made him want to be better inside. Where it counted.

Don't miss
Amish Jane Doe *by Shelley Shepard Gray,*
available August 2022 wherever
Love Inspired Suspense books and ebooks are sold.

LoveInspired.com

LISEXP426093